A HOWL LOT OF LOVE AND LIES!

A TAMSIN KERNICK ENGLISH COZY MYSTERY

BOOK 9

LUCY EMBLEM

First Edition 2025

Published by Quilisma Books

ALSO BY LUCY EMBLEM

More mysteries with Quiz, Banjo, and Moonbeam

Where it all began ..

Sit, Stay, Murder!

Ready, Aim, Woof!

Down Dog!

Barks, Bikes, and Bodies!

Ma-ah, Ma-ah, Murder!

Snapped and Framed!

Christmas Carols and Canine Capers! A Howling Good Christmas Mystery!

Game, Set, and Catch!

A Howl Lot of Love and Lies!

The Charity and Muffin Cozy English Mystery series

A Tail of Village Murder

CHAPTER ONE

Tamsin's hands were full of shopping bags and dog leads, as, turning to glance up at the mighty Malvern Hills looking down protectively over the town of Great Malvern this May morning, she pushed open the door of The Cake Stop with her backside and allowed the equally well-laden Emerald to pass through.

"Look - there they are, over there!" said Emerald, and they threaded through the tables to deposit all their bags against the wall behind the table in the window, where Andrew and Sara had gathered some armchairs together in anticipation of their friends arriving.

"Oh, hello Quiz!" Andrew stroked the big collie's dark head. Then, "Moonbeam, good to see you!" He greeted the little black and tan terrier with the delicate legs and tiny paws. Moonbeam stood up on her hind legs very prettily and pirouetted for him. "No Banjo today, Tamsin?"

"He's not mad about crowds, so he's happier at home this morning."

"Is there anything left in the Farmers' Market?" quipped Sara, looking at the bulging bags.

Emerald grinned, "A fair bit - but Charity was cleaning up after us. She'll be here in a moment," she added, delicately winding her long legs up under her as she relaxed into the armchair.

"Susannah was giving out samples of her newest goats' cheese - it's gorgeous!" said Tamsin as she subsided rather more heavily into the next armchair with a satisfied sigh, settling Quiz and Moonbeam on the mat she'd put down for them. "So creamy ... Hey, are you off from College now?" she asked Sara.

"Yes, Daddy came over with the horse box and we brought Crystal home this week. I'm looking forward to lots of long rides in our beautiful Herefordshire byways and bridlepaths this summer. I hope it'll be a good one!"

"They do say it's going to be warm," agreed Andrew, tearing himself away from gazing at Sara to turn his boyishly enthusiastic freckled face to Tamsin. "When I'm off work I'll be borrowing one of the hunters from the estate and joining Sara."

"We're going on a walking and climbing holiday in Wales too!" said Sara, her eyes shining.

"Sounds as if you've got your summer sorted - Oh, look who's here!" said Tamsin as the door swung open and in strode the tall and rangy figure of Feargal, the young reporter who was always in a hurry. She gave a great wave, and noticed Emerald blushing slightly, letting her long blonde hair fall forward over her face and looking more than usually demure.

"Who hasn't got a coffee?" said Feargal, generating a fizz of energy, having reached their table in a couple of long strides.

"I'll come up to the counter with you," Tamsin gathered herself and got up from the chair, "Give you a hand."

"Ogle the cakes, you mean," laughed Feargal, as they headed towards the counter - where Jean-Philippe was busy working the gleaming coffee machine with its noisy milk frother - and admired the display of gorgeous cakes.

"I'll do more than ogle them," Tamsin smiled as they joined the short queue. "Look at that one," she gasped, eyeing a fluffy concoction of cream and meringue, "And that chocolate cake is to die for!"

"That's probably what you *will* die for," mused Feargal with a grin, as they moved to the head of the queue, "the amount of cake you put away."

Tamsin pouted. "I eat very well - most of the time. The Three Furies' cakes are my one slip from healthy eating."

Feargal snorted, "'The Three Furies'! Who coined that name for Dodds & Co in the first place?"

"I don't know .. It may have been me, but I can't remember. Three indomitable sisters with Ancient Greek names ... But you have to agree their cakes are divine?"

"They are. But I see you've got lots of good stuff from the Farmers' Market too," conceded Feargal, then leant towards her and said, "I was only teasing, gal."

"*Mes amis,* what can I get you this morning?" the deep voice of Jean-Philippe boomed over the counter.

"*Bonjour* Jean-Philippe!" chorused Tamsin and Feargal together. "No Kylie today?" added Tamsin.

"*Mais si!* Kylie is very much here. She is just filling the dog water bowl specially for you."

"That's very kind of her - I do appreciate it. But they just had a good glug as we stopped at the spring at the Elgar steps, so they're ok for now. Very popular, that spring. I had to wait behind someone who was filling four big plastic drums from the fountain."

They placed their orders and Kylie bounced in from the kitchen saying, "I'll bring those over for you!" As they went back to their seats Feargal saw the small figure of Charity coming through the door.

In one bound he held the big glass door for her. "Come on, Muff-muff!" said Charity, and smiling sweetly at Feargal she immediately stopped to greet some of the other regulars in the café. Feargal waved his card at Kylie. "Can you add a pot of tea for one, and whatever Charity would like to eat?"

"Feeling expansive today? Got a bonus for your investigative articles?" teased Tamsin.

"Charity is a marvel, and should be encouraged at every opportunity," he smiled. "I'm still hoping to get her to write a column for us at the *Malvern Mercury,* on the Malverns in days gone by."

"You're right - it would be a cracker! Her memory is unbelievable."

"I don't think much can have happened over the last seventy years that Charity doesn't know about," agreed Feargal.

"And it gives her such insight into today's issues. For her, there's nothing new under the sun!"

They settled down with their drinks and cakes. Emerald dimpled her cheeks sweetly when Feargal passed her hers. Tamsin avoided staring at them by attending to Quiz and Moonbeam, who were now excitedly greeting Muffin as Andrew pulled up another armchair to accommodate Charity.

"Oh, thank you dear! How lovely to see all you young things here together." She paused, then leant across to Tamsin and said quietly, "How's Jonathan doing these days, Tamsin?"

Now it was Tamsin's turn to dimple. "He's up at the Farmers' Market touting his organic cider to all comers. He can't get away from the stand, but I'll probably drop by again on my way home." Then she plunged a large spoonful of lemon meringue pie into her mouth, to forestall any more questions from Charity. She was not used to talking about herself.

"So!" said Sara. "What are you all doing this summer? Going away anywhere?"

"It's such a long time since I went away anywhere," said Charity with a sigh, "apart from visiting my niece in Torquay with her new baby. When I was a child we used to have the most wonderful bucket-and-spade holidays in Bognor Regis or Bournemouth. We even went down to Woolacombe in Devon one year. Lovely big beach there."

"You're right! I took the dogs there when I was down the West Country a couple of years ago - it's three miles of golden sand, and mostly empty!" enthused Tamsin. "The exhausting bit was having to haul yourself up the ropes on the deep-sanded dunes when you leave the beach." She smiled at the memory. "So you went to lots of seaside towns?"

"We did. It rather depended on the train service, you see. My family never had a motor car. Farm labourers didn't."

"You'll be staying at home this year and attending your garden, I guess?" said Emerald soothingly.

"Well, Dorothy had an idea of us doing some outings. Now she's on her own with the two dogs she's feeling a bit constrained, especially with her B&B guests. There's that nice garden centre towards Gloucester, there's the Worcestershire Art Trail to explore, and I thought I could visit Hereford Cathedral again. I haven't attended a service there for years!"

"Be sure to go before the choirboys go on holiday!" said Tamsin. "I heard the three Cathedral choirs singing together at the Three Choirs Festival once. They were divine!"

"Did you know that the Three Choirs Festival has been going for three hundred years?" announced Feargal, between crunching mouthfuls of his toasted sandwich.

"No, really?" said Sara.

"Yes, it's always based on the three Cathedrals - Hereford, Worcester, and Gloucester. What?" he paused and looked at the others gazing at him. "I wrote an article on it, didn't I. That's how I know." And he continued munching his toastie.

"Well, there's a bit of history for us!" said Andrew. "I have to admit to being a bit of a philistine - though I do admire those three Cathedrals."

"Mummy usually gets a season ticket for the Festival," said Sara. "We'll have to purloin it and go this summer."

"So that's two of us sorted out," said Charity, stroking Muffin, who had scrambled onto her chair. "What about the rest of you?" She looked pointedly at Emerald.

Feargal decided to chance his arm. "It's the silly season for news, so I'll be able to get away alright. In fact," he hesitated for a moment then carried on, talking fast, "a friend of mine has offered me his house in the Pyrenees. I'm hoping to go for a few days."

"How lovely!" said Emerald. "I've always wanted to go to the South of France .."

"Wanna come? Weekend in the mountains? Yoga on the terrace in the baking sun?"

Emerald looked uncharacteristically flustered for a moment, till Tamsin jabbed her leg with her foot under the table. "Yes, that would be lovely!" said Emerald with a broad smile.

Tamsin could see Feargal's shoulders relax, and gave a secret smile to

Charity for so cleverly engineering this breakthrough. But she was brought up short by Sara.

"So there's just you, Tamsin?" Sara leant forward eagerly.

"Oh well, you know me," she shifted in her chair. "I don't like to go abroad because of the dogs. A holiday's not worth it if I can't take them too. And *Top Dogs* is flourishing. I have a waiting list and classes running all summer ..."

"That's impressive, but you could take a cottage somewhere!" said Andrew. "I'm sure there are lots of dog-friendly places?"

"I could," said Tamsin doubtfully.

"It would do you good to have a break, dear. You work so hard running your dog training school," said Charity.

"And I guess Jonathan won't be tied up with the apple harvest for a while yet?" Sara teased with a sly smile.

Tamsin decided it was time to change the subject.

"Hey, I have news!"

They all turned to look at her, while Feargal started in on his second plateful of food.

"You remember the Valentine's Day thingy that Saffron organised back on um .."

"February 14th?" prompted Sara with a grin.

"You mean the one that got cancelled at the last moment because of the fire at the hotel?" asked Charity.

"Yes, that's the one. Poor Saffron was so disappointed."

"Who's Saffron?" asked Sara, looking from face to face.

"Ah," Tamsin paused to think. "She's a student of Emerald's. And she kinda backed the wrong horse and got landed with a baby and no support. But that .. shall we say .. got resolved in the end, and she's trying to get her business going again."

"For now she works for Linda in *Health in the Hills,*" added Andrew.

Sara nodded, realising there was slightly more to this story than Tamsin was letting on, and that she'd have to wait for another time to hear the rest.

"Anyway, she'd sold quite a few tickets for the February event and had to give all the money back. Of course, the hotel refunded her booking fees, but she'd put an awful lot of work into it."

"Such a shame," said Emerald. "I think it was great that she decided to branch out a bit. It must be hard juggling baby Charlie and her shifts at the health shop."

"And her design business! Rotten luck for her," agreed Andrew. "We'd got tickets."

"I'd been looking forward to it! Wearing a pretty dress instead of jodhpurs, back protector and helmet, for a change," grinned Sara.

"And mud!" quipped Andrew.

"Well, it looks as though you're in luck. She's got over the shock and upset and decided to go again."

"For next February?"

"No! That's just it - she's having a 'Midsummer Valentine' evening. She's got some farmer over Halfkey direction who's going to rent her a field which is not on the side of a hill. She's going to have a marquee!"

"I hope said marquee will have a floor, so we're not dancing round cow-pats!"

"Oh, she's getting the works. And it will actually work out better than the hotel. Manic will be DJ-ing."

"Manic? Your hedgehog-saving friend?"

"That's the one. Apparently he does this on the side - I had no idea. Jonathan tells me he has great taste in music. I wouldn't know."

"Oh yeah," said Sara, "they became friendly over the sad collapse of Jonathan's little old Ferguson tractor, didn't they? Manic being a wizard mechanic by trade? I've met him at the bike shop when I've been doing my Saturday stints. He's friendly with Mark there, too."

"That's right - that's how we first met him, through Mark. Well, Jonathan and he are very chummy. Unlikely pair ..." Moonbeam hopped up onto her lap, balancing her tiny feet on Tamsin's thighs. "Anyhow, she's getting in touch with everyone who bought tickets. And I said we'd help."

"You did?" Feargal's fork paused mid-air.

"Saffron's so delightfully scatterbrained - she needs encouragement! I said we'd help spread the word. We can dish out flyers. Perhaps you can get something in the *Mercury*, Feargal? They did report on the fire before."

"You're absolutely right," said Charity firmly. "It's so good that you offered - you always see the best in people, dear. Saffron does so well with that little boy of hers, and her yappy little Napoleon too. We should give her a hand."

"She's giving a lot to charity too - not this one," she patted Charity's knee with a smile, "the Malvern Mothers or something - single mums, you know."

"'Malvern Mothers'?" Charity frowned. "Do you mean 'Malvern Homemakers'? They're awfully good, you know."

"Oh, is that where you do your cookery classes, Charity?"

"I just help out there sometimes. Some of the girls are so young they don't know anything about housekeeping or cooking - or even how to use a washing machine, some of them." She shook her head sadly.

"'Malvern Homemakers' then," Tamsin shrugged. "It's on the flyers anyway."

Andrew suddenly exclaimed, "Oh, that's what Linda was on about! You know Linda owns the health shop where Saffron works," he explained to Sara. "I didn't really follow ..."

"I see you listen to your landlady as much as you listen to me!" Sara teased.

Andrew ran his fingers through his short ginger standing-up hair and grinned. "Yes, she was talking about the event and ... and ... something else." They all laughed.

"So are we up for helping Saffron?" asked Tamsin.

Everyone nodded. Feargal made a note in his phone about the announcement, and the girls fell to chattering about what they would wear on the night, leaving Feargal and Andrew to talk about more manly things.

CHAPTER TWO

"What are you up to today?" yawned Emerald as she floated down the stairs, her luscious long-haired cream cat Opal doing her usual dot-dot-dot down the stairs in front of her.

"Hi! It's a rare day when I'm up before you," Tamsin indicated the cafetière she was filling and Emerald swished her long blonde hair over her shoulder and said, "Yes, please!"

"Let me see .. it's Monday," Emerald added as she began to dish out Opal's food. The cat, who had been prowling the worktops since arriving downstairs, tucked her legs and tail neatly under her and purred raucously as she ate. Forgetting that she'd asked Tamsin the question, and choosing to answer it herself, "So that means I have two private lessons. One this morning and one this afternoon."

"It's a gorgeous day today, first signs of real heat in the sun. I do like May - everything beginning to burst forth and blossom ... Like to join me for a trot on the Common? I'm meeting Manic there at 3. He loves spending time with the dogs."

"Bit more cuddly than his spiky hedgehogs! Oh thanks," she took the mug of coffee Tamsin held out for her. "My afternoon session is at half past three up in town, so yes - that would be perfect!"

"I've got a home visit this morning too - then, of course, there's the Nether Trotley Tricks Class this evening."

"What tricks are they learning now?" asked Emerald as she carried her mug and bowl across to the table.

"Well, Chas's boys are teaching Buster to crawl. Then he can join in their games when they're soldiers creeping through the jungle," Tamsin smiled at the thought of Cameron, Alex, and Joe, and what fun they had with their little Jack Russell Terrier, Buster. "Susan's trying to teach Frankie a roll over. He kept rolling on her flower beds so the idea is to teach him to roll over only when she tells him. It's a bit chaotic so far - legs everywhere. And not just Frankie's! Then Shirley is teaching her great big Luke to pull a little cart contraption." Tamsin finished waving her arms about to describe the scene, and brought her own mug and bowl to the table too.

"Not too heavy for him?"

"I think it would need to be quite solid to be too heavy for a Great Pyrenees! He barely notices it. She got her son to make it for her."

"Mark, from the bike shop? Of course! Handy, having a mechanic who knows about wheels in the family!"

"Then there's the poodle doing her pirouettes, and the two dachshunds playing dead. One goes right over on his back - it's very comical!"

"What's Charity doing with Muffin?"

"Ah, now, Charity. She did so well teaching Muffin to pull her sleeves to help her get her coat off, that she's teaching her to pull her socks off too."

"Regular little assistance dog Muffin is becoming!"

"And of course Charity's not getting any younger ... so I think she'll find these tricks genuinely helpful." She took a mouthful of oats and raspberries as she gazed out of the window at the sunny garden. "They do so love doing these things. There's always a scramble to see which of mine will bring me a sock first in the morning. Banjo's usually the winner. It's quite comical when Moonbeam decides she saw the sock first and they have a tug-of-war with it!"

"You must get through a lot of socks that way."

"Haha, no - they're very good. They get all my old socks anyway, as toys. Just wash them and tie a knot in them and they go into the toy basket." She licked her spoon and plonked it into her empty bowl with a flourish.

"Waste not, want not!" grinned Emerald, as the three dogs gazed at her, wondering if she may drop a morsel of her breakfast their way. She didn't, of course. She was on pain of death to feed dogs from the table, and had learnt this rule very early on when she first came to live at Pippin Lane.

So it was much later that day when they all set out for their walk on the Common, Emerald wearing a straw sun-hat and looking like a film star - except for her backpack with a big yoga mat sticking out of it - and Tamsin with her three dogs' leads attached to her walking belt.

"There he is, leaning against that Chestnut tree!" exclaimed Emerald as they rounded the corner and the great expanse of verdant common-land opened up before them, beginning to give off warmth from the after-noon sun.

And sure enough, there was Manic, as ever in a sleeveless t-shirt which he wore whatever the weather, his wiry tattooed arms folded in front of him, the chains and sharks-tooth pendant round his neck glit-tering in the sunshine. A small figure against a mighty tree.

"Wotcher, Tamsin!" he called out. "Hey, Emerald - you too?"

"Oh, I'm just sharing the walk up to the top road. I'm off to town to earn a crust."

"Good for you! Let's walk up that way together, then." Manic greeted the three dogs as, one by one, they were let off their leads. Quiz and Moonbeam were very pleased to see him, and showed it.

"Banjo still a bit cautious round you, Manic," said Tamsin, as she reassured her shy grey collie.

Manic squatted down and gazed into the middle distance, letting one hand dangle over his knee while the other was flat on the ground. Banjo stretched his neck forward and sniffed gingerly at the hand nearest him, then snuffled and got a bit closer, his tail beginning to wag softly, low down.

"Hey Banjo," Manic said quietly as he turned his face slightly to the dog, being careful not to stare at him.

Banjo suddenly identified this person as a friend he'd met before but in a different place, and reached up to sniff his face, his tail now wagging furiously, and his mouth slightly open in a smile.

"There you go!" said Tamsin, "It's your friend Manic. Did you not recognise him in a new place? You had to get his scent?"

And they set off up the hill together to walk Emerald nearer to her lesson.

"How's business for you these days, Tamsin?" asked Manic.

"It's just brilliant! All my classes are booked up, with a waiting list. I do lots of home visits, which are such fun. I just wish I had some land where I could teach tracking and search & rescue .." She shrugged. "Maybe one day. But really, I don't think my life could get any better."

"Wanna bet?" said Emerald mysteriously.

Tamsin stopped and stared at her friends. "Why are you both looking at me like that?"

Manic glanced at Emerald, then said, "We're just pleased for you, that's all. It all sounds terrific!" and he took the twig Moonbeam had brought him and tossed it aside for her to find again.

As they split up at the top of the Common, where the top road was cut into the side of the Malvern Hills, Tamsin put Moonbeam back on her lead again.

"Why do you do that?" asked Manic as he waved to the retreating figure of Emerald, now walking away on the top road, her yoga bag bobbing behind her.

"Moonbeam loves Emerald, and she may think she's a sheep escaping from the flock, and needs to be brought back. We're too near the road for any shenanigans like that." They walked back down the hill. "I'll be able to let her off again soon," she assured him. "I've brought their frisbees, want to play?"

"Sure! 'Their frisbees'? They each have their own?"

"Yep. Don't want them racing after the same one and having a mid-air collision. They know exactly which is theirs." As they stepped through a gate into a large enclosed area of the Common, Tamsin demonstrated by throwing first one frisbee, then the next, collecting the first one delivered back to her as she threw the third.

"You look like some kind of demented windmill!" laughed Manic. "Which one will I throw?"

"You take Quiz's - she's not quite as fast as the other two, and I bet you can throw miles further than I can!"

Manic's first throw for Quiz went quite the wrong way, leaving Quiz puzzled as she looked this way and that for where it could have gone.

"It's all in the flick of the wrist," explained Tamsin, and showed Manic a few throws.

"Got it," he said, and it wasn't long before Quiz was panting hard, chasing after his long-distance throws. "Need some water, Quiz?" asked Manic.

"Let's give them a drink in the stream and we can stay in the shade for a bit," suggested Tamsin. "It's surprising how warm this late spring sun is, once it breaks through."

So they walked down a shaded avenue of splendid beech trees and sweet chestnuts, the frisbees stowed in Tamsin's walking belt and the dogs happily snuffling in the undergrowth.

"It's lovely to see them - just being dogs," said Manic. "They are a delight to watch."

"I'm glad you can enjoy their beauty too. Hey, I hear you're DJ-ing for Saffron?"

"The 'Midsummer Valentine' - I am, indeed. She'd booked someone for the February event and had to pay his fee as the cancellation was so late. I won't charge her for it. I think it's great that she's trying to make some money out of running events. Rather her than me!"

"How do you know Saffron?"

"Mark met her at a photography class - the one you were at, remember?"

"How could I forget?" said Tamsin with feeling, as she remembered the unfortunate Carruthers sisters.

"Ah yes, another of your triumphs! I've met her a few times since, at clubs and the like. She's good fun! And how do *you* know Saffron?"

"Oh, we go back quite a way. She was in Emerald's yoga class when … that awful thing happened to one of the other students. She's been through a lot. It was on one of my group dog walks that she met Linda, and got work at the health shop."

"You're a regular networker! And how are you involved in the Midsummer Valentine?"

"Like you, really. I think Saffron deserves a bit of support. I'm just helping where I can - bit of publicity, flyers, you know the sort of thing."

"Will you be coming to the event?"

"I think so. I'm not really into dressing up and all that, though."

"I'll see if I can find 'How much is that doggy in the window?' to play for you," laughed Manic. "You're definitely into 'waggly tails'," he added, watching three tails waving together as the three noses were deep in a bush.

CHAPTER THREE

A couple of weeks later, Tamsin arrived home from a very wet walk to see Feargal's car outside the house in Pippin Lane. She came squelching into the house with the three dogs. It was pouring rain, and once she'd dried them all and despatched them to their beds, she dived towards the kettle, rubbing her hair with a towel. 'That should have given them time enough to notice me,' she thought.

The living room door opened and in came her two friends, both with slightly flushed faces. Quiz and Moonbeam leapt off their beds to greet them ecstatically - as if they hadn't seen them for about a hundred years. Banjo watched cautiously from afar.

"Coffee?" asked Feargal. "Sounds like a plan."

"Here, I'll do it," said Emerald. "You look pretty wet - want to change?"

"Yeah, I will, thanks. Got caught in an April shower that was a few weeks late. It was lovely when we went out! You got class tonight, Em?" she said, as she climbed the stairs.

"Yes, my usual one at The Cake Stop."

"I was passing, so I thought I'd give her a lift up there - seeing as it's so wet," said Feargal, stepping from one foot to the other. "Too wet for the bike .."

"Right," said Tamsin, smiling to herself, and disappeared into her room for dry clothes.

By the time she came downstairs again, her nose led her to the living room, where the cafetière was filling the house with its warm aroma. Tamsin went in and flung herself into an armchair with a sigh, pushing the damp hair out of her eyes.

"That was a good piece you did in the *Mercury* for Saffron," she said to Feargal. "She was delighted with it!"

"Has it produced the goods?"

"It has. Lots of signups. And somehow I've got lumbered with the ticket list. Still, it makes interesting reading - look," and she reached for the sheet of paper on the mantelpiece.

"Let's have a look who's coming!" Emerald shuffled forward in her seat eagerly, dislodging Opal from her lap. The cat scowled at her and strutted away, tail erect like a flagpole.

"There's some people from the Nighthawks mountain biking group - see? There's Adam, who seems to have captured the heart of Cynthia after all, and Johnny Lightholder."

"I guess Mark Bendick must have put flyers in the bike shop."

"*Flying Pedals*? Yes, I believe he did. He's coming himself, so perhaps he needed a bit of support."

"Mark's bringing a girl!" Emerald pointed at the list.

"Ooh, let's see .."

Tamsin looked at the entry. "Cassandra, she's called. I believe she's a new Nighthawk."

"And Johnny Lightholder, you say?"

"Yes - that should be entertaining. He's bought two tickets, but I don't know yet who's going to be the lucky girl."

"He'll have to use all his powers of persuasion!" giggled Emerald.

"Who else is there?" Feargal pulled the sheet slightly so he could read it too.

"Julia, from Bishop's Green. She must have told the rest of the tennis club, because look who else is coming," and she pointed to some names below Julia's. "Glenda and Toto, Neil Allardyce - he's the Club Secretary - and Victoria, and Coach Gavin, and Amanda!"

"Goodness! I hope there won't be any fireworks from that lot," said Emerald.

"I'll look forward to seeing Glenda in evening dress," mused Feargal with a crooked smile. "Wonder if she'll wear tennis shoes under it ..."

"Presumably Saffron will seat them all at the same table. I'm not party to the seating arrangements, thank goodness."

"Playing with fire, that!" agreed Emerald. "Ooh, look at this," she indicated a couple more names.

"Niamh O'Connor and Tiernan," read Feargal. "Wasn't she that teacher?"

"Yes, the one young Cameron had a crush on. She's nice."

"So what's Saffron up to if you're handling this list?"

"She's coming round this evening, as a matter of fact. On her way back from *Health in the Hills*. Linda's been giving her more hours now she's found a reliable childminder for Charlie."

"That's good," mumbled Emerald, checking the time.

"So - we'll see tonight!"

"Oh, look at the time!" Emerald bounced up from the chair. "I'll just run up and get ready," and so saying she ran up the stairs.

"Got anywhere with your Pyrenees Party?" asked Tamsin.

"Yes! We've fixed the dates. It'll be lovely there - can't wait." Feargal looked just like Opal when given a dollop of cream.

"It sounds wonderful. I think you'll have a great time - all that French food .."

"And coffee! You should go sometime. They like dogs - they go to restaurants and everything. My friend - the guy who has the house - has quite a few dates available when he's not using it himself."

"I just may take you up on that one of these days ..." and Tamsin was interrupted by Emerald appearing in the doorway in her stretchy gear and carrying her yoga bag.

"Ready?" she asked.

"Ready! Let's go," and the two of them left the house. In the quiet that followed, once the dogs had settled again, Tamsin heard Feargal's car start and move off. "Bless them," she said, to whoever may be listening. "They've found each other at last. Yes, Banjo," she added, as Banjo came over and rested his chin on her knee, "we knew for ages before they did."

Then clearing up the coffee things, she tidied the place a little, played some games with the dogs, and was ready for Saffron when she arrived.

Saffron cascaded through the door, her mop of black curls flying, dropping her bag as she bent to greet the dogs, filling the house with her energy and presence.

"Ooh, can you smell Napoleon?" she asked excitedly of Moonbeam, as Tamsin retrieved her dropped bag and stuffed the spilled items back into it. Who knew what the dogs may pick up, in this jumble of papers, hairbrush, nappy pins ...

"How's Charlie?" Tamsin congratulated herself on remembering what she was meant to say first, though she was really more interested in Saffron's little dog Napoleon than in her baby.

Saffron straightened up with a huge smile. "Oh, he's wonderful!" she said. "He's beginning to babble, and he can crawl so fast! He tipped over Napoleon's water bowl the other day - everything was soaked!"

Recalling the untidiness of Saffron's house and garden, Tamsin said, "It must be hard to childproof everything?"

"Oh, I believe in freedom. So long as it's not actually dangerous, then Charlie must explore as much as he likes. I have to say, Napoleon has turned up trumps. He's fascinated by Charlie, but no, I know what you're going to say! They're never left alone together - not even for a moment, and I don't ever let Charlie pull the dog around. That would be so unfair, and he has to learn to respect everyone, beetles, dogs, or people." She stopped to draw breath, and Tamsin took her opportunity to invite her over to the table and offer refreshment.

"No thanks, Tammy," said Saffron, completely failing to notice Tamsin's teeth grinding at the unwanted nickname. "I had coffee at the health shop café. And a bun, oops!" she patted her shapely tummy. "Let's look at what we've got so far - it's so exciting!"

Tamsin found that getting Saffron to keep her thoughts on track was a bit like herding cats, so she adopted her dog trainer approach and got her to deal with just one item at a time.

Saffron had most of the necessary things in hand. She'd impressed the farmer up at Halfkey - especially as his niece had once been in the family way herself, and the charity had been a cause close to his own experience. The marquee company was booked and was delivering flooring as well. "There's going to be some sort of non-slip matting for most of it, then a section of wooden floor near the DJ for dancing. It's too expensive to floor out the whole tent. Look!"

"I can imagine!" said Tamsin as she studied the glossy brochure from the marquee company. "Manic is looking forward to it. I didn't realise you knew him."

"We met at the photography class exhibition. He came to see Mark's photos one day when I was there. Some of Mark's photos were of him riding his motor bike. And actually he often comes into the health shop to pick up some grains for his rescued hedgehogs. He prefers to get organic stuff from us than whatever they have in the pet shop."

"That would be Manic, alright!" smiled Tamsin.

"He's a bit of an acquired taste for some people," said Saffron sadly, "you know, the way he looks, with his black hair, bare arms and chains - and bones in his ears and all that - but I think he's lovely."

"He affected that look to protect him from being bullied - not being all that tall. They make a funny twosome - Mark with his fair curly hair, looking for all the world like a big friendly farmer, and little dark, wiry, Manic ... but you're right - he's a softie."

Saffron leaned forward and said in a confidential voice, "You know he's not charging me anything for DJ-ing? What a lamb!"

"He told me. Think he's glad of the opportunity. You can rely on Manic to do things right."

"He came round the other evening to go through the music. Charlie *adored* him! In fact, they looked beautifully matched, with their olive skin and mops of black hair." Saffron gazed into the middle distance.

"Charlie has a mop of black hair now?"

"He does! Love it ... ooh, he's going to be a heartbreaker when he grows up," she giggled.

Tamsin thought, 'like his Dad,' but didn't say it - and decided to get back to business. "Now, let's look at these ticket sales ... Got your copy?"

"Yes, here it is." Saffron rummaged in her crammed bag, frowned, then rummaged some more. "It *was* here .. Sorry - can we use yours?"

Tamsin went and fetched her list from the living room and spread it out on the table.

"There's some more to add!" Saffron said excitedly. "A surprise 'nother one from the photography class .."

"Not Oliver, the tutor?" Tamsin gaped, wondering if he might arrive in a green dinner suit with orange tie.

"No, not Oliver - Janice Carruthers, you know .."

"Estelle's sister. Well, goodness me. It's good that she's beginning to get out and about again. Who's she bringing?"

"This is the amazing bit - you know that nice Sergeant at the station? Well, it seems that when he was handling her during all that - all that - well, *all that* - he rather fell for Janice. They're an item!"

"What an amazing case of 'All's well that ends well'! Well, I never .. Any other surprises?"

"I don't think so. There are people you know there, I'm sure, and plenty we don't know at all. Yet." Saffron gave a deep sigh. "Do you know, I always believed in love? Love will find a way. Love will out .. That's why I so wanted to get this Valentine's event going again." Saffron gazed intently at Tamsin. "'Midsummer Valentine'. Doesn't it just sound *so* romantic?"

"I'm afraid I don't have a romantic bone in my body," said Tamsin placidly. "But I'm happy for you, Saffron. You deserve to find someone nice to be with you and Charlie, you really do. But you'll have to choose rather better .."

"Don't I know it! Once bitten, twice shy, I always say." She gathered her papers together and pushed them back into her bulging bag. "Now I must fly, or the childminder will murder me!" She got up and moved toward the door. "And you're right. Charlie deserves the very best. I will have to choose ve-e-e-e-ry carefully," and so saying, the whirlwind that was Saffron disappeared through the door.

Though not without catching her sleeve on the handle and having to detach herself, with a giggle.

CHAPTER FOUR

"Look at those Fieldfares!" exclaimed Charity, hastily calling Muffin back to her.

"Is that what they are? I've never seen them before - and such a lot of them!" Tamsin put her three dogs in a down so they wouldn't disturb the grazing birds.

"They're winter visitors, dear, members of the thrush family."

"Ah yes, I see their speckledy breasts now."

"Actually, they're here late this year. They're usually gone around Easter. Must be this funny weather we've been having."

Tamsin and Charity were enjoying a walk in a nature reserve near the Malvern Hills. Nowhere around the Hills could be described as flat, but these slopes were definitely less steep than the Hills themselves, and it was a nice change for Charity, who sometimes found the ascents a bit challenging these days.

The weather was glorious for May. Bright, clear, fresh, and apart from them and their dogs, the fields were empty. The hedgerows were bursting with blossom and bright green leaves and hosted a lot of bird activity. Tamsin sighed with pleasure as she surveyed her surroundings.

"Let's go through this gate into the next paddock, and leave the birds to it," said Tamsin, unlatching the gate in the tall hedgerow.

And as they stepped through the gate a new vista opened up before them, of the southern end of the Malverns.

"There's Midsummer Hill!" said Charity, pointing.

"And Perseverance, and Pinnacle Hill!" Tamsin pointed further to the right, then fastened the gate and admired the view. "Just can't quite see British Camp - it's behind that beautiful ash tree there."

"And just look at this field full of buttercups - the dogs are loving bounding through them!"

"You're right," chuckled Tamsin as Banjo ran back to check she was coming. "And just look at you, Banjo - your white chest is all yellow!" she laughed as they trudged on.

"Is your young man going to the Midsummer Valentine with you?" asked Charity, raising an eyebrow mischievously.

"Not you too, Charity! Emerald and Feargal are forever teasing me about him. We're *friends,* that's all."

"Tell it, as they used to say, to the marines. I've seen how he looks at you. And, he certainly looked after you during that tennis club fiasco!"

"He did. You're right. He's very sweet."

"Sweet and smitten," Charity said quietly. "And you knew who to turn to in your moment of need."

"True. And I do like him. But, you know, as Saffron said to me the other day, 'Once bitten, twice shy'."

"From what I saw of your Sebastian you both rather rushed into things. And him disappearing was probably a good thing, as it turns out. At least you kept the house."

"And the mortgage!"

"You've known Jonathan a while now. And you're right to be cautious, my dear." Charity walked on a good few yards in silence, then turned to look at her friend. "But is he coming?" she grinned.

"Alright, yeah, he's coming," Tamsin grinned back. "Along with a lot of other people. Saffron's got quite a big crowd coming. I know some of them, of course, but by no means all of them."

"I came across a new person who's bought tickets - um, Raymond something? No, Ronald. Richard? Rex? No no, Michael - that was it!"

"Your filing system malfunctioning, Charity?" giggled Tamsin.

"I knew it began with an R," the old lady smirked back.

"Anyway, he's new to the area and is bringing his wife. They're from Worcester."

"How did you meet him?"

"It was at the Library. You know I do a sort of reading class for the Adult Literacy people?"

"I had no idea, Charity! You never cease to amaze me. I only hope I have half your energy when I get to your age."

"Grey hair doesn't mean a grey brain," Charity laughed. "Look at our friend Dorothy and what she gets up to!"

"Absolutely! She's bounced back so well from .. you know. I'm hoping my natural curiosity will keep me young in my dotage."

"Assuming you get there. You are pretty reckless at times," Charity tutted. "Well, to get back to Michael - after the class I was at the desk and he was asking about clubs and societies in Malvern so he could get to know people, being a newcomer. So, of course, I told him about the Midsummer Valentine. I had a flyer in my bag, so I gave it to him."

"Well done!"

"Seems he's working for the Council. Not sure what at ... Here, shall we turn down this path?"

"Yes! I can see a pretty little wooden bridge over the stream down there, and it shouldn't be muddy at this time of year."

The path wasn't muddy, but there was plenty of standing water either side of it in this carefully-conserved wetland. Tamsin groaned as her dogs sploshed and splashed through it, their paws getting blacker with every bound. "Good thing I have a hose at home," she sighed.

"They're loving it."

"That's alright for you to say. Little Muffin is keeping right by you so she doesn't get muddy!"

Charity beamed at her little, clean, dog. "So who else new is coming, dear?"

"Have you met the new couple in the sub-post office in West Malvern?

"Oh yes, in the pub. Let me think .. Marjorie, and um .. Bertie, no - Brendan .."

"Harold."

"Harold, yes, that's it. Knew it began with a B."

"Charity, you're incorrigible!"

"So they're coming?"

"Yep. And thinking of shopkeepers, there's Steve and Dottie from the Link. Remember them, from the Carol singing?"

"Indeed I do. And you may get another shopkeeper. Ned - the butcher up in town. I see him quite often when he's delivering to the single mothers' place."

"So you buttonholed him?"

"I did. These people *should* support a local event - especially when it's for a local charity."

"Fair enough." Tamsin noticed that Charity was beginning to slow down. "Hey, how time flies when you're enjoying yourself! I have to get a move on. Let's cut back through this gate - that'll lead us straight back to the cars."

"Right you are, my dear. Come Muffmuff," and they returned across a drier field to their vehicles.

"In you get, dogs," said Tamsin, opening the back of the *Top Dogs* van. "Straight to the hose in the back garden for you lot!"

CHAPTER FIVE

"Bonjour Mesdemoiselles!" boomed the deep voice of Jean-Philippe as he held the door of The Cake Stop open for Charity with Muffin, and Sara, who'd bumped into each other on the way down the hill. "Your friends are already *la-bas*," he added, pointing to the window table and armchairs. "Kylie will look after you this morning," and with a bow he stood aside for them to go to the counter.

"How perfectly charming you are, Jean-Philippe!" said Charity, squeezing his hand as she passed.

"Tea for one, Charity?" said Sara brightly. "I got paid this week, let me get this - anything to eat?" and she gestured Charity towards the table where Tamsin and Emerald were already holding court, Quiz and Feargal in attendance.

Once greetings were performed, tails wagged, and chairs pulled up, Tamsin said, "We were just saying that it seems there's a sick person about."

"Oh no, not again," Charity looked dismayed.

"Yeah. Seems that a couple of people have received out-of-season poison Valentines."

"Poison Valentines?" queried Sara through a mouthful of cake.

"Ooh, what have you got?" Tamsin interrupted herself as she caught sight of Sara's laden plate. "Is that the Toffee Tango?"

"I don't know what it's called, it just jumped out in front of me and said 'Eat me!', so I said, 'If you insist'."

"I simply couldn't resist the Coffee Walnut today. I don't know what the Furies do to their cakes, but they are out of this world ..."

"Tamsin!" Charity called her to order.

"Oh sorry, yes. Valentine cards with nasty messages in."

"What sort of messages?"

"The one Niamh O'Connor got said, 'You've got no hope'. And there was an even nastier one which said 'Trying to catch someone before you're too old and ugly?'"

"No!" gasped Sara. "Who was that sent to?"

"Janice Carruthers."

"Oh, how mean! The poor woman's just recovering .." said Emerald, shaking her head.

"You know there's nothing new under the sun?" said Charity quietly. "They talk about people making nasty remarks online under the cover of a false name, don't they?"

"Trolling," said Sara.

"Well, I can remember when I was a child, people were still talking about 'Vinegar Valentines'."

"Vinegar Valentines?" asked Tamsin, looking up, eyebrows raised, as she took her last spoonful of white icing with a walnut perched on top.

"Nasty messages in nasty cards. They were often crude, apparently. Very common in Victorian times." Charity smoothed her skirt across her knees and shrugged, "Of course, I never saw one. But the idea of sending anonymous nastiness just doesn't go away, does it?"

"People are so weird!" agreed Sara, "Such a waste of energy. I mean, if I *really* wanted to be mean to someone, I'd want to see the effect it had on them." She looked at everyone staring at her. "But I wouldn't, of course!" she said quickly, and dived back into her Toffee Tango.

"It's a funny time of year to be sending Valentines," said Emerald thoughtfully.

Feargal, who had been working his way quietly through a plate of toasted sandwiches, wiped his hands and said through a mouthful of crunchy crumbs, "Both those people had bought tickets for the Midsummer Valentine."

"You're right!" Charity passed two small pieces of biscuit to Muffin and Quiz. "Somebody knew."

"Somebody did indeed know," agreed Feargal. "But we don't yet know how. I mean, obviously it wasn't Saffron or Tamsin, who have access to the guest list."

"Oh!" Tamsin put down her mug. "I think we *do* know how. You remember how scatterbrained Saffron is?" Most of them nodded. "When she came round the other day, she'd lost her copy of the guest list. I didn't think anything of it at the time - just assumed it was on her kitchen table with sploshes of tomato soup on. Her bag was stuffed full and over-flowing - maybe she dropped it somewhere in town, or at the health shop?"

"So someone's picked it up and is now sending vicious messages to people on the list?" asked Emerald.

"Laughing at them," Feargal shook his head sadly, glancing at Emerald's bowed head.

"How did you hear about them?" asked Sara. "I mean, if I got something like that I'd probably keep it to myself."

"Me too!" agreed Tamsin. "But you know Janice is seeing that nice Sergeant?"

"Really? How perfectly sweet!" said Charity.

"Seems he got attached to her during that investigation." Tamsin nodded in agreement. "And he'd also got a report from the headmistress of Niamh's school, who was feeling very protective of her young teacher. So he's logged their complaints."

"But how did *you* know?" Sara persisted.

"Walls have ears," Tamsin smiled and glanced at Feargal.

"I pick up the odd titbit from the police station," he said quietly.

"Ah yes, I seem to remember you having inside information before," Sara nodded knowingly.

Feargal coughed loudly. "Now, who's for a refill?" he said, as Kylie, with her pink hair and pink micro-mini-skirt approached the table with a tray.

After top-ups had been ordered and squabbles about who would be allowed to pay had been resolved - it was decided that as a student, Sara shouldn't be paying much at all, till she assured them that she could - "Daddy gives me an allowance!" she declared proudly - they returned to the subject of the poison Valentines.

"Where can they be getting them from at this time of year?" mused Sara.

"Now that's an intelligent question!" said Feargal approvingly. "They must have stashed them away in February .."

"Unless they're someone who has access to out-of-season greetings cards .."

"You're right, Em!" Tamsin jumped forward in her seat. "There are two that I can think of. There's Steve and Dottie - remember them, with the little newspaper shop down in the Link?"

"Oh yes, from the Christmas Carol-singing," Charity piped up, as she adjusted Muffin's elbows in her lap. "Here Muffmuff, you're pressing on my, er - *Muff!*" she squawked. Feargal snorted into his coffee and Sara giggled quietly. Charity looked at them in puzzlement. "Young people ..." she sighed.

"Yes, them." Tamsin chose to ignore the hilarity. "And there's the new sub-postmaster in that pub in West Malvern. They'd have Valentine cards, presumably?"

"Perhaps they would. I don't know them - they're new aren't they?" asked Emerald.

"Yes, they are. Charity, can you remember their names?"

"Benny. No, Barnaby .. begins with a B. Brian .. Harold! That's it! Harold and Marjorie."

Everyone smiled fondly at Charity. "You have a strange way of getting there, but you always do get there in the end! And you're better at remembering names than I am," laughed Tamsin, making space on the table for Kylie who had returned with their coffees. "I'll have to go and check out this sub-post office, see who they are."

"But it could be anyone!" objected Sara. "Anyone could have bought them back in February, and .. and .." She frowned.

"*Maybe*," said Feargal brightly, "maybe they were going to do it last February, then when the fire happened and the event was cancelled, they didn't." He shrugged. "For some reason."

"And what reason could there be?" asked Emerald, who always had difficulty understanding the warped minds of people whose intentions were bad.

"There's only one reason I can see," said Feargal slowly. "They were going to lead up to something at the original Valentine's event, but perhaps they didn't know who'd bought tickets, so they didn't send them."

"Or, they did send some and no-one admitted to receiving one. I mean, they *are* nasty."

"You're right, Sara. Like you, I'm sure I'd keep it to myself if I got one."

Feargal spoke out, "We must all say, if we get one now!" The friends all nodded in agreement.

"And keep the envelope!" said Charity.

"But, if that's the case - that it's connected to the cancelled event - does this mean they're planning to do something now, at the Midsummer Valentine?" Emerald's mouth stayed open in shock at the thought.

Tamsin looked grim. "We need to stop this before then. It'll break Saffron if her event is ruined for the second time. Feargal, can you find out how the police investigation is going?"

"Sure," he nodded. "And you can check out those two card-shops."

"Right you are."

"Keep your ears to the ground, everybody," said Feargal. "We need to nip this nastiness in the bud!"

"Oh dear," Tamsin chewed her lip. "I have a feeling this could end badly."

CHAPTER SIX

The next morning Tamsin parked up one of the side roads in Malvern Link and paid a visit to Steve and Dottie's shop. As ever the shopfront was busy and garish, the window covered in orange stars with slashed prices. And as ever, apparently regardless of the season, there was a tub of children's colourful footballs parked out on the pavement.

Tamsin went in and looked at the greetings card rack while Dottie gossiped with a customer.

"So I says to 'er, I says," Dottie proclaimed loudly, "If that's what yer thinking, you can sling yer 'ook!"

"Quite right, Dottie old girl. You don't want to put up with any nonsense from the likes of 'er! Just this paper today, dear." The customer held out a handful of coins and waved her paper.

A smile tickled Tamsin's lips as she remembered the last time she'd crossed swords with Dottie, the devoted cockney wife of her ex-army husband Steve. Dottie was nothing if not forthright!

Rooting around in the cards as the conversation went on, she found plenty of birthdays, anniversaries, school-leaving, and baby cards. But nothing seasonal. No Easter, Christmas, or Valentine cards. So absorbed was she that she didn't notice the customer leaving till the bell on the door jangled.

"Can I 'elp you with them cards? Special occasion, is it?" Dottie was actually being a model helpful shop assistant.

"Oh, hi Dottie!" Tamsin turned to her with a beaming smile. "Tamsin. Remember? From the Christmas Carols."

"I don't want to remember them Carols. But yeah, I remember you alright. Bit of a busybody, wasn't you."

"I'm sorry I came over that way, Dottie! It was all so awful, wasn't it. Getting roped into a murder like that .."

"Din' I see something in the local rag about you?"

"Oh, I write a column there every so often - on dog training. It's what I do."

Dottie had lost interest and her eyes glanced longingly at her crossword puzzle book on the counter, which she'd put aside to chat to the previous customer. The person who'd actually bought something. "You want a card then?"

"Well, I know it sounds odd, but I was wondering if I could get a Valentine's card?"

"You've missed the boat on that one, dearie. They're gorn."

"You don't save them for next year?"

"Nah. The 'olesaler takes 'em back. They'd get all scruffy if they was left there for a year. There's no call for them after the day." She picked up her pencil and opened her puzzle book.

"That makes sense. So I can't get one. Hmm. Has anyone else been in looking for them?"

"Not so's I noticed."

"Do you know anywhere else might have them?"

Dottie filled in a word then scribbled it out. "Nah, don't fit," she muttered.

"Let me see," Tamsin leant over the counter and read the clue upside down. Remembering that Dottie wasn't protective about her puzzles as long as she could fill them in, she read aloud, "'Mathematician at a warm time of year.' Try 'summer'."

"Ow, that's it! Thanks dearie." And as Tamsin opened the door, setting the bell jangling, Dottie called out, "Ain't no-one gonna have Valentine cards now. You'll just have to cut out a big red 'eart and stick it on a card yerself."

Chuckling, Tamsin closed the door and went back to the *Top Dogs* van, mentally charting a course to 'The Pig and Sparrowgrass' in West Malvern. After listening to Dottie's London Cockney, it was nice to think of the Worcestershire dialect that called the asparagus grown locally in the Vale of Evesham 'sparrowgrass'.

It was a glorious late May day, perfect for admiring the views from the Malvern Hills. And as Tamsin drove through the Wyche Cutting - the ancient salt route cut through the rock between Malvern and Colwall and beyond - she marvelled as ever at the vista that opened up before her. The landscape sparkled in the sunshine, and she decided to pull over to take in the view properly.

The fields and clumps of woodland swept all the way to the hills in the distance, the Black Mountains in the Brecon Beacons National Park in Wales straight ahead, shimmering pale blue as they met the even lighter blue of the sky. When she'd learnt that they had been named the Black Mountains by the Saxons because they always viewed them from the East - against the sun - she felt a deep fellow-feeling with her ancestors, though she certainly had Celtic blood in her veins too, the Celts who had lived the other side of those Black Mountains. In her case, it was the Celts from the South-West, Devon and Cornwall.

Over to the right she could see the dense green of Bromyard Downs, and thought of the many dog walks she enjoyed there.

"No dog walking this morning," she said with a sigh to her empty vehicle, and slipping the car into gear, she glided out onto the hill descending in a wide sweep along the western flank of the Hills into West Malvern.

West Malvern had houses on the hill side of the village that had steep gardens climbing up the side of the Malvern Hills. While on the valley side, the houses had no visible gardens as they dropped away - often in steps - below the houses.

"No good for dogs, these gardens," she muttered, as she thought with pleasure of the flat - though small - garden behind her little house in Pippin Lane. She pulled up near The Pig and Sparrowgrass, with its pretty sign hanging still in the windless air. The road was narrow and she tucked her van in tight to the kerb, remembering to flip her wing mirrors in as she got out.

Having a sub-post office in a pub wasn't that common, and Tamsin was curious to see how it worked. Not liking the smell of beer-stained carpets herself, she was pleased to find that once through the heavy dark wooden doorway of the old pub, the air inside was fresh and pleasant. It was still early - before the usual pub opening time of 11 o'clock - but there was a soft buzz of conversation from three villagers enjoying a coffee at one of the tables.

"Well, this is different!" she said to the middle-aged barmaid who was chalking up the lunch menu on the blackboard.

The barmaid turned with a welcoming smile, "Looking for a coffee, or the post office? We don't open the bar till 11."

Spotting the splendid espresso machine, Tamsin said, "I'd love a coffee!" and perched on a bar stool as the woman set about making it for her.

"I haven't been here since you took over, I think? You've certainly made a difference!"

"Thank you! When we arrived we found the village had no post office, no shop - in fact nowhere for people to meet. It's a shame that all these people live cheek by jowl and don't ever get to meet each other!"

"Very enterprising," Tamsin nodded. "I guess it helps pay the bills too?"

"We get people coming in now who would never have come when it was just a pub." She lowered her voice. "Those ladies over there run a knitting group here on Wednesdays."

"I seem to remember there was a skittle alley at the back of this pub?"

"There was, lovey. But no-one plays skittles any more. So we put a snooker table and pingpong there. Very popular with the kids at the weekend!"

"Quite the local hub! I'm Tamsin - I live the other side of the Hills."

"I'm Marjorie, pleased to meet you." Marjorie extended a limp hand over the beer taps. She turned back to finish the noisy business of frothing the milk, then handed a pretty pottery mug of coffee to Tamsin.

"Oh, that mug's from a local pottery, isn't it! I've seen them at the craft market in Great Malvern."

"We have to support local artists too," beamed Marjorie. "This potter actually lives in West Malvern! We have pictures on the walls too sometimes, as exhibitions, like."

"I'm very impressed." At that moment a large red-cheeked man came shuffling into the back of the bar, lowering a jangling crate of bottles to the floor.

"Just changed the barrel, love," he said to Marjorie.

"Harold, this is Tania,"

".. er, Tamsin," said Tamsin.

"Would you listen to me!" laughed Marjorie, giving Harold a friendly shove in the ribs with her elbow to cover her embarrassment. "What am I like?! This is *Tamsin*. It's her first visit to The Pig and Sparrowgrass."

"You're very welcome, Tamsin. I hope you enjoy your coffee. There are some books about the Malvern Hills over on that shelf, if you need any reading matter."

"Thank you. I'm being very well looked after. Are you thinking of adding a shop too? I visited the West of Ireland once, and there all the pubs had shops in them. Quite the normal thing."

"Sensible idea. We're thinking of it. It would have to be that small area over near the door," he gestured to a dark space at the end of the bar by the post office counter, before slipping away again.

"I'm sure you'll manage it." And seeing there were no cards or suchlike on sale in this particular post office, Tamsin took her coffee to a table, picked up a book from the shelf, and sat down facing the door and the bar.

As the clock ticked round towards 11, a noisy vehicle rattled to a halt outside the pub, the door was thrown open and a large man stooped slightly to enter through the low door of the pub. He was wearing country tweeds and stout, grimy, working boots and sported a large, bushy, grizzled, moustache. "Morning all!" he said cheerily, clapping his hands then rubbing them together. "Time for my morning snifter!" Marjorie shook her head, saying, "You'll have to wait a few more minutes, my duck, if you don't want us to lose our licence. I could hear you coming a mile off! When are you going to get a decent car?" Marjorie smiled at him.

"That there's a proper farm vehicle, I'll have you know. But I'll be driving a swanky Merc soon, you wait and see." The big man finished his sentence with a great guffaw, looked round the pub and his gaze alighted on Tamsin. "Ah, a visitor!" he crowed, as if he'd found a fresh victim.

He stood in front of her table. "I'm William Lett," he proclaimed, "but you can call me Bill, everyone does!" He cackled mightily. The three ladies in the corner paused for a moment, gave a sidelong glance, then carried on their quiet conversation.

Tamsin looked up at the blustery jolly man with his big moustache and instantly thought of Major Cooper-Johnson in Bishop's Green with all his model archery animals. "Good morning, Bill," she said obligingly.

Bill stood up straight and clicked his heels together in response. She amended her thoughts - 'Actually, more like Colonel Simkins from the carol-singing, who also lives in the last century .. but one'. She opened the book on the table and made as if to start reading.

Marjorie noticed her discomfort and called out, "Come over here, Bill, you old reprobate. What are you having this morning?" she nodded her head to the clock, which was just reaching the hour. Pulling his pint, Marjorie said, "How are the preparations for this Midsummer event then, Bill? I must say it's very brave of you to use your 50-acre for it. Won't the cars mess it up?"

"It'll be fine - just so long as we don't have a summer thunderstorm and the cars all get stuck in the mud," he guffawed loudly at the thought. "I'll have a tractor on standby if they need it. Farming these days - you have to *diversify*, Marjorie old girl. That's the word they use for making money where you can. Diversify. An' I have some great plans for *diversifyin'*." He winked and tapped the side of his nose. "You'll see me driving that Merc yet, Marj!"

"And pigs might fly .." retorted Marjorie with a laugh.

Tamsin, rescued, thumbed through the book and thought about life, while Bill brayed and chortled through his chat with Marjorie. 'So that's the farmer renting Saffron the field.' And she fell to thinking about diversifying and what the farmer and this enterprising pub couple were doing with their businesses.

It's interesting how people adapt, she thought. Things change all the time, and you have to move with the changes or you get stuck. It can be hard to part with the past. But forward is the only way to go, or you get stuck in the mud and need a tractor to pull you out.

She wondered why she was thinking these thoughts right now, when she should be thinking about poison Valentines.

She had no dog to keep her company but the coffee was good. It seemed that Harold and Marjorie were a positive pair, and she couldn't imagine them doing anything as nasty as sending messages like that to someone they didn't know. As for Bill Lett, that sort of thing didn't seem to fit in with what she could see of his character.

Perhaps the card-sender did know the people he - or she! - was writing to. Or perhaps he was using a scattergun technique, and was actually targeting one person, but covering his tracks with all the other cards?

And only that one person may know the true venom behind the messages.

Tamsin shuddered despite the sunny day and the warmth of the cosy pub. What was this person planning for the Midsummer Valentine?

CHAPTER SEVEN

Tamsin put her key in the door at Pippin Lane and heard a big nose snuffling and snorting at the crack in the doorframe on the other side. She smiled in anticipation as she came in and was greeted excitedly by her dogs.

"It's ok! I was only gone an hour or so," she chuckled, as she gave each of them a hug. And feeling magnanimous, she also ran her hand down Opal's back and gave her tail a slight tug. Opal loved this, and came back for more, smarming the side of her face against Tamsin's hand before presenting her tail for another pull.

Flinging the garden door open, Tamsin stepped out into the sunshine. "It's a lovely day," she told her crew. "Let's eat outside! I have to get ready for Puppy Class in Malvern in a minute."

She was just starting to assemble crusty sourdough bread, goats' cheese and salad, when Emerald came in, hanging her yoga bag on the newel post. "Just in time," said Tamsin, cutting more bread, then getting out another plate and mug, eliciting a big smile from Emerald.

"I was giving a private class in the upper room at The Cake Stop this morning," said Emerald, once they were sitting at the picnic table in the garden, enjoying their lunch. "And when I came down I was waiting to talk to Jean-Philippe about dates, and there were three women in the queue."

"Yeah?" Tamsin swept some crumbs off her lap for her politely waiting dogs to hunt for in the grass, which seemed to need mowing yet again.

"One of them had picked up a flyer for the Midsummer Valentine, and she was saying, 'I hope my ex isn't going to be there, that would spoil everything.'" Emerald took a sip of her coffee. "Then one of the others said, 'I don't mind who's there as long as I don't get put on a table with ..' some name I couldn't hear. But then the third woman, bit younger than the others, put on a dreamy expression and said, 'I can't wait!'"

"Interesting. I hope they're not disappointed! I gather there's another load of tickets been sold since the last list Saffron sent me."

"It looks as though it'll be a huge success!"

"Only if we can find out who's sending these nasty cards. I had no luck finding any today. Apparently - according to the indomitable Dottie - 'there ain't no call for 'em', so they return them to the supplier till next year."

"It's as we thought then. The sender must have got them for the first Valentine event, and hung on to them."

"Pretty weird."

"Deranged, I'd say."

"That means he - or indeed she - could be dangerous."

"I've got a nasty feeling about this, Tamsin. You will take care, won't you? I mean, I know how much you love this detecting, but .."

"You're very sweet, Emerald," Tamsin put her hand out and covered her friend's hand. "Maybe you're right. Maybe I should let the police deal with this .."

"Oh my! I didn't expect you to *agree* with me!" Emerald's face was a picture!

"I think perhaps I'm mellowing in my old age. I've got a funny feeling that everything's about to change."

"Something in the warm weather, perhaps?"

"It is beautiful, isn't it," Tamsin looked up towards the Malvern Hills

- the familiar dark shapes against the bright blue of the sky - and sighed. "I love my life, and what I do. *Top Dogs* is going so well. But I've been content in this life for too long. I can feel change approaching."

"How philosophical you're being! But I think I know what you mean. Life is a series of ascending steps - with plateaus. You move forward, then you take stock and settle in for a while. Like me settling in Malvern. I don't know if that's for ever ..."

"Well, I hope we don't go too far apart, Em old thing," Tamsin smiled at her.

"And I hope we keep living in a wonderful place like this. I'm very fond of your little house here."

Tamsin leaned back and closed her eyes against the sun for a few moments, then jumped up. "Time for Puppy Class! Come on, gang," and they all betook themselves back indoors.

CHAPTER EIGHT

Tamsin's class bags were packed ready in the spare bedroom which doubled as her store-room, so it took no time to fetch her box of treats from the fridge, pick Moonbeam to accompany her today, and set off to her Puppy Class.

It was always one of her favourite classes. The big round eyes of the little puppies, taking in everything in this strange world they'd landed in, and the pride of their new owners - usually already besotted with their pup - never failed to cheer her, even in the bluest of moments.

But today she was feeling cheery and happy. She laid out her wares on the table, and put Moonbeam's mat on a chair so that she wasn't at the mercy of all the puppies as they dragged their owners into the hall.

Although it was still ten to the hour, her teaching began straight away, as the excited students filed in.

"Just unwind the lead from your hand, Mary - let Pedro have a bit of choice."

"Oh isn't Millie walking prettily in her new pink harness!"

"Give Barney some space there, everyone, you know he's very shy .."

And gradually they all settled themselves down, putting their bags down by their chairs, setting out the mat they'd brought for their puppy, sorting out their treat pouches and some toys, and chatting to their neighbour.

"Look how quickly Jasper is settling on his mat!" said Tamsin to one of the owners. "Well done - you've been doing your homework .."

"I can't quite believe how calm Jasper is when the mat appears! Only last night I ..."

But their conversation was interrupted by a squawk from Mary. "Ohh! Oh, how horrid!" Pedro pawed at her leg, as his Most Important Person was clearly upset. Tamsin hurried over.

"What is it, Mary? Whatever's wrong?"

Mary was holding a hankie to her face with one hand, and dangling a card in the other. "I was rushing to get here, so I grabbed the post as I left. I've just opened this." She held the card up to Tamsin, her face full of distaste.

Tamsin's heart sank. It was a Valentine card, adorned with love hearts. "May I?" she said, about to open it.

"Go ahead, but it'll turn your stomach."

Tamsin opened the card, sensing the hush around her from the rest of the class. Her face paled as she read the words inside.

You stupid old harridan. Who could ever love you?

"You're right, it's horrid. And you know what you should do?"

"You should burn it!" said one of the other students.

"Oh no," Tamsin said firmly. "Put this card and its envelope in a bag - I'll get you one from the table - and take it to the police."

"Oh, I don't want to trouble the police .."

"But you should. You see, Mary, you're not the only person to receive one of these poison cards."

There was a gasp from the rest of the room, who then became animated and said, "Yes, Mary, you should!" "Can't let sick people get away with this sort of thing," and the like.

Tamsin took the card and holding it and its envelope by the corner went over to the table and slid them into a plastic bag. "Can you take this down after class, Mary? Promise me you will."

Mary gulped and nodded. "If it stops someone else getting one, then I will. But it's so embarrassing!"

"You've nothing to be embarrassed about! It's not your fault there's someone with a screw loose. Hey," Tamsin spoke more quietly, though the rest of the class was now buzzing with chatter, "are you going to the Midsummer Valentine by any chance?"

Mary blushed. "I am, as a matter of fact. My old friend whose wife died last year - he invited me. It'll be nice for him to get out. Ernest used to love going to dances with his wife."

"You may mention that when you leave that in at the police station - about going to the Midsummer event," Tamsin said thoughtfully, then went back to the front of the room and called everyone to attention.

"Now, everyone, it's your fourth class, so you've got a lot of the basics. And to turn our mind to happier things," she beamed at the puppies - some chewing a toy, some sitting on their owner's lap, some gazing at her in wonder - "we're going to teach them some tricks today!"

There were oohs and aahs and some giggles, and the class switched their attention back to their puppies.

Tamsin explained how simple they'd find it to teach a trick, now that they had the foundations in place, and pointed out that the trick had to suit the individual dog.

"I know Jasper there is going to be a large dog, and right now he'd probably find a Roll Over hard. Does he ever lie on his back? No? Then he may enjoy 'Bang! You're Dead'. He only has to lie on his side for that one."

Jasper's owner laughed, her eyes shining in anticipation of teaching him the trick.

"Millie, on the other hand, is small, so she's used to stretching up - look, she has her paws on your knees now. So I think she may suit a Sit Pretty - a sit up and beg!"

Tamsin worked through the class, suggesting to each owner what may work best with their individual puppy. Then she invited Moonbeam to hop down from her chair and she demonstrated how to teach each trick, all broken down into little steps.

"Remember that you won't be adding the vocal cue till the action is almost right. Just like you didn't say 'Sit' till your puppy was sitting every time. Your word will be describing what the dog is doing. 'That thing you're doing? We call it a Spin', sort of thing."

From then on, the room was filled with happy chatter and laughter, as the owners focused on getting the actions they wanted, and the puppies tried to work out what it was that was being asked of them. Some well-timed tips from their tutor got things going surprisingly fast, and by the end of the session, nearly all the puppies had a good grasp of their trick.

"Let's see them all doing it perfectly for your final class - you've got a couple of weeks to work on this,"

And while the group were packing up their things, Tamsin went over to Mary to reassure her again, and to encourage her to go straight down to the station with the beastly card.

"Really, Mary. It's nothing to do with you, the police know that. Just some sicko wanting to hurt people generally."

And once the hall was empty and quiet, Tamsin did a bit of recall training with Moonbeam - whose recall was excellent but could always do with a refresher - then stacked the chairs, swept the hall, and gathered her own gear together.

"You aced those tricks, Moonbeam! Let's go," she said, as she locked the hall door. "I have more to tell Feargal when we get home. I wonder if he has anything to tell me?"

CHAPTER NINE

Back at Pippin Lane, Tamsin and Moonbeam greeted Quiz and Banjo. "Your turn for some training tomorrow, Banjo old bean."

"What are you doing with him now?" came a voice from the stairs as Emerald and Opal wafted down in a cloud of silky cream - fur for Opal and a long floaty summer dress for Emerald.

"Oh hi, Em. More cadaver training."

Emerald pulled a face. "I still can't believe you can get the scent of dead bodies in a bottle to spread on the ground ... yuk!"

"Better than having to rob a grave, wouldn't you say? It's one of the conveniences of modern dog training," Tamsin grinned. "I'll be taking him to the little paddock tomorrow to do a bit of searching. He does love it."

"No other dogs or people to worry him?"

"Exactly, although when the people are all wearing orange hi-vis suits he's ok. He knows they're the rest of the Search & Rescue team, and he's always pleased to see them. And they him!"

"I can understand why - he does look cute in his orange hi-vis vest! So how was class?" she asked as she washed a couple of mugs for the cafetière Tamsin was making.

"Oh, I have to tell you! In fact, I want to talk to Feargal too. Is he coming over today?"

Emerald was wide-eyed. "No?"

"I'll give him a buzz." Tamsin picked up her phone and starting texting the young reporter. "You see, there's been another poison Valentine."

"Oh no! How perfectly horrid."

"Hang on while I get this coffee going and I'll explain."

They adjourned to the garden and Tamsin detailed the events at Puppy Class. "I'm hoping she did go to the police station. So you see, we need to get moving. Ah, there's a reply from Sonny Boy .." And she read the message. "He has news too. I'm just asking him to come round." Her fingers moved swiftly as she texted. "Have we a fatted calf we can kill?" she asked with a smirk, knowing Feargal's gargantuan appetite.

They fell to deciding on what to make for dinner, and shortly before Feargal was due, Emerald unaccountably needed to go to her room to do her hair. Quite what she would do with her long straight ash-blonde hair was a mystery to Tamsin, who raked a comb through her dark mop once a day and felt it more than enough. But Emerald did look very fetching when she came down the stairs again, a comb holding some freshly-picked daisies at the side of her head.

Feargal certainly seemed to think so, judging by the rapturous expression on his face when he arrived and saw her, as he waded through the welcoming swirl of excited dogs.

"We're up to five now," he said, as he plonked himself on the sofa next to Emerald.

"Five poison Valentines?" asked Tamsin.

"Yes. I gather you sent one person to the cop shop with hers."

"Poor woman," sighed Emerald. "Such a nasty thing to do."

"The police can't do much with just the cards. *We* have to do something," said Tamsin.

"Wouldn't there be fingerprints?" asked Emerald.

Feargal turned to her, "Only smudges so far."

"Can't they find out where they were posted or something?" she asked.

"They've done that." Feargal began to explain. "But they all caught the first post at different post offices in and around Malvern. So he'd have all night to sneak to any postbox and post his cards. They can't put CCTV on all the postboxes, and there's nothing to be seen on the film they've checked from the post offices themselves."

"So they're a bit stuck," said Tamsin with a sigh. "But we're not!"

"What are you thinking, old gal?" asked Feargal.

Tamsin scowled at the 'old gal' then said, "Well, we're thinking they're sending cards only to people who have tickets for the Midsummer Valentine, right?"

The others nodded.

"So they must have got the list, as we thought, to know."

"Ye-e-e-es," said Feargal slowly, beginning to follow.

"You can only buy these cards in February. They must have bought them for the first Valentine event, the one that was cancelled. So let's get the previous list - the one for February - from Saffron - and see which names are the same."

"I get you! We can at least maybe narrow it down a bit." Feargal enthused. "If they bought the cards back then, they must have had some victims ready."

"I'll get on to Saffron right now," said Tamsin, and reached for her phone. Their conversation was interrupted by, first, Napoleon screeching at the window as a horse and rider trotted past their house; then a wailing from Charlie who'd dropped his favourite bear; and then a cry of "Hang on, the pan's boiling over!" from Saffron.

But eventually, from the chaos that seemed to reign in her house, Saffron was able to say that she'd locate the previous ticket list in no time. "I had to refund everyone, remember? I know just where it is. Twenty minutes. Can you give me twenty minutes? I need to get Charlie's dinner sorted." Then as an afterthought she added, "But why do you want it, Tamsin?"

"Well, er, there've been some unfortunate happenings."

"No! What?" said Saffron with alarm.

"Oh, don't worry about it. It's just that some of the people who are planning on coming to the Midsummer Valentine have had some, er, nasty Valentine cards."

"Nasty?"

"Nasty messages. The police are following it up, apparently, because they reported them. I just wondered .. You see, you can't buy Valentine cards at this time of year, so I thought maybe someone bought them for the original event, but once it was cancelled, they didn't send them then. I know it sounds weird. But maybe they were working off the first list of ticket-buyers?"

"Oh Lord, Tamsin. This will finish me if it all goes wrong again. I'll have run right out of money. Oh Lord!"

"Listen Saffron. We're going to sort it out. Your event will go fine. Don't worry about it. Twenty minutes?" Tamsin reminded her, then finished the call and translated for the others, "She'll email it in an hour. Let's eat."

Over their meal they fell to discussing Feargal and Emerald's forth-coming trip to the Pyrenees.

"I can't wait to go to one of those wonderful French markets," enthused Emerald. "All that cheese!"

"Don't they have more varieties of cheese than anywhere else?" asked Feargal.

"Ah, now *that* I do know about!" Tamsin jumped forward in her chair. "I was talking to Susannah at the Farmers' Market one time - you know, the goatkeeper?"

The others nodded.

"She said that there are actually more varieties of artisan cheese in the UK now than there are in France!"

"Wow!" said Emerald. "Anyway, the markets will be wonderful. If only our Farmers' Market had tables groaning with fresh local peaches and lemons!" Her face was shining.

"And baguettes and croissants," sighed Tamsin.

"You getting your Jonathan away for a holiday, Tamsin, old thing?"

Tamsin pulled a face. "He's not 'my Jonathan'."

"Well you *have* been out with him a few times .." Emerald remarked.

"He's good company, I grant you. And we've had some nice walks in his orchards with all the dogs." She tossed her hair back from her face. "But I'm not looking for anyone at the moment."

"You got burnt with that guy ..?" Feargal asked gently.

"Sebastian," Emerald provided.

"I did. Not feeling too trusting. Anyway, Jonathan's good company, as I say, and he's planning on coming to the Midsummer Valentine."

As Tamsin reached for her phone to check her mail, and bent to stroke Quiz's head at the same time, Feargal and Emerald exchanged glances.

Eventually, long after they'd finished their meal, Saffron came back with the old list.

"Can't think why I couldn't lay hands on it straight away!" she wrote, as she emailed it through to Tamsin, who would have been very surprised if she had.

The lists weren't long, so Tamsin and Feargal took one each and ticked off any people they could exclude - like themselves and Charity, Sara, and the new people who'd only just signed up.

"That still leaves a lot of people on both lists," observed Emerald, looking over Feargal's shoulder and adjusting Opal's paws so she could lean towards him.

"It does. It does indeed .." Tamsin nodded. "Ok, let's get stuck in. People we don't know first."

Feargal ran his pen down the column and read out, "Tiernan, Niamh's teacher friend. Hilda's husband Alfred."

"If he's anything like Hilda we can probably discount him," said Tamsin.

"Not yet. Let's look at everyone," he reaffirmed, then went on, "There's Lucinda's partner Jefferson."

"Oh, I saw them in The Cake Stop the other day. Very lovey-dovey." Emerald said. "He looks like a latterday hippie - grey pony tail, wizened beard, you know? I wouldn't have thought he was Lucinda's sort ..."

"Martin Bramwell's bringing someone."

"Surprised he can show his face," snorted Tamsin. "Is it the same person as he had down for February?"

"No name provided, just 'plus one'."

"He sails a bit close to the wind. Wonder who the lucky lady is .."

"Hmm. There's a party of the Nighthawks coming."

"Nah," Tamsin dismissed them. "Can't see it. Those mountain bikers are only interested in speed and self-destruction."

"There's Ned the butcher and Mrs. Ned."

"I really can't imagine him doing anything nasty," protested Tamsin. "Though I don't know his missus."

"Leave him on the list," cautioned Feargal.

"There's the tennis club crowd, but we know all of them - for better or worse! They play all hours at this time of year. Surprised they can tear themselves away from the courts for a dance! But they feel they owe us, I think, after what we did at the club. That's the impression I got when I was playing there on Wednesday." Tamsin grinned and chewed her pencil as she read. "What about this Michael geezer, who's recently moved here?"

"Yes, there's him, and that couple you met in West Malvern," said Emerald, stroking the purring Opal.

"I happen to know Michael is putting in for planning permission to make a huge house with gym and swimming pool and the works out of the medium-size one they've bought," said Feargal, tapping his teeth with his pen. "Council must pay better than I thought!"

"Or perhaps he has money from somewhere else .. his wife perhaps?"

"We need to know more about them."

"The couple in West Malvern - Marjorie and Harold - appear to be good eggs. Trying to become the heart of the village, you know?"

"It's hard to tell when someone is secretly deranged," sighed Emerald, affectionately twiddling Opal's whiskers. Opal lay with her face upturned, eyes closed, softly purring, enjoying the attention that was her due.

"Oh, there's one more," said Feargal. "Rosie's boyfriend. Both lists. I guess Saffron dragooned them into coming, seeing as Rosie works at the health shop. I expect she'll scrub up well!"

Tamsin sighed and put the list down on her lap, for a moment forgetting that Moonbeam was already occupying said lap, so the sheet floated down to the floor. She scooped it up, saying, "Thing is .. what does this guy -"

"Or gal!" said Emerald.

"You're right! What does this male - or female - hope to achieve with these poison cards? Is he going to go for something dramatic at the event? Is he aiming at someone in particular - perhaps someone who rejected him?"

"Or her," Emerald repeated.

"Or her - though all the cards we know of so far have been sent to women. Perhaps they're just wanting to be a spoilsport?"

"Or something worse." Feargal shook his head sadly. "I don't think he - or she," he nodded to Emerald, "will be satisfied with just secretly posting things. I think he'll -" he held up a hand and nodded, "I think he or she will want to witness their victim's discomfort."

"As sick as that?" Emerald paled.

Feargal smiled as he found a way round the he/she thing at last. "I think they're warming up to something."

CHAPTER TEN

"Mais bonjour, au Maître Créateur de Cidre!" Jean-Philippe greeted Jonathan with a solemn bow as he held the door open for him.

"New handle for me, Jean-Philippe?" Jonathan chuckled, plunging his hands into his pockets.

"Master Cider-maker!" Jean-Philippe clarified. "That is you, *hein?*"

"It is!" laughed Jonathan. "I like that!" He clapped the barista on the shoulder as he looked around for Tamsin.

"They are there in the window, as usual," Jean-Philippe said quietly. "You can spot them amongst all the dogs," he grinned.

Jonathan, looking like an eager young puppy himself, bounded over to greet his friends. Though he really had eyes for just the one. "Hi Tamsin, thought I'd snatch some time off from the market and join you for coffee."

Tamsin smiled in response. "Who's minding the stall?"

"Manic! He was up scouting for discarded cabbage leaves at the veg stall - for his hedgehogs, you know? And he spotted you and Emerald leaving with full shopping bags and, guessing where you were going, he offered."

"Good old Manic!"

"He's a find - and not just for mending antique tractors! We get on well."

"Good man to have in your corner," agreed Feargal. "What are you having? I guess you're in a rush?"

"Oh, thanks, I am! Just a quick espresso then I have to dash back." Jonathan took Feargal's vacated seat as he took the order to the counter. "That's jolly decent of him," he remarked to Tamsin.

"Gave him a good excuse to go and get more food!" she grinned, as Emerald nodded too.

"I don't know where he puts it all," said Charity, who had been fussing over settling Muffin and Quiz beside her. "He must have hollow legs. He's as thin as a rake. All you young men are," she sighed, admiring Jonathan's slim physique.

"Hard work is what does it," he said. "Though I'm sure you're no stranger to hard work yourself, Charity?"

"It's kept me occupied for many a long year," the diminutive old lady smiled back at him. "But it's beginning to catch up with me, at last."

"No, surely not!" chorused Tamsin and Emerald.

"What's this?" asked Feargal, returning with a tray laden with plates of food and Jonathan's coffee. "Here you are, old man." He passed the tiny espresso cup and saucer to Jonathan as he pulled up another chair.

"I always think those cups and saucers look like they come from a dolly's tea set," smiled Charity. "And that shows you how old I am," she sighed, "I doubt they have dolly's tea sets in video games these days." And then she held up her hand to forestall any more protests about her being old. "I'm thinking my life may change soon."

"Charity!" Jonathan inclined his head and spoke quietly. "Are you trying to tell us something?"

"Oh, no, dear! I'm not ill or anything. No, no - I feel very well, thank you. But I think it's time for me to do some of the things I've always wanted to do but never thought I'd have the time for."

"Like going on safari?" Feargal's eyebrow raised cheekily.

"Nothing so grand, my dear. I'd just like to spend some idle time visiting old country houses and their splendid gardens. Looking at works of art. Learning more about the natural world. I was thinking of doing a course in the University of the Third Age or whatever they call themselves these days. There's all these things that I've always been too busy to fit in."

"Well, you do so much charitable work, Charity - living up to your name!" laughed Tamsin. "Perhaps it's time for someone else to share the load?"

"Trouble is, there's nothing I want to give up. I love working with young people, as you know. So the knitting class at the after-school club suits me well. And it's so rewarding helping people to learn to read, at the Library."

"That's where you met me!" said Tamsin. "Though I could read already," she added with a grin.

"Aren't you involved with the church too, Charity?" asked Emerald.

"I just help with the smaller children at choir. That's not difficult. And they look enchanting in their red and white choir-dress ..."

"It *is* very rewarding, yes - working with young people," agreed Jonathan. "I enjoy taking the children's summer camp at Tom's Tennis Club. They keep you young!"

"Oh, they do!"

Jonathan turned to Tamsin, "Forgot to tell you, those three scallywags of yours have been signed up for camp this year."

"My three scallywags? Oh, you mean Cameron, Alex, and Joe!"

"The same."

"They're such fun! Lovely family - I'm glad they're coming along."

Charity nodded, "Lovely family indeed. Young Alex has energy for at least five boys."

"So what *are* you going to change?" asked Jonathan, turning back to Charity. "The trouble is you love doing all these things."

"That's what has me in a quandary!" replied Charity, dislodging Muffin from her lap in her enthusiasm. "Oh sorry, Muffmuff!" The little dog hopped back up and gave her owner's hand a forgiving lick. "I'm going to have a chat with Dorothy about all this. She's very wise, you know, though she doesn't show it."

"Oh, indeed she is!" Tamsin turned to Jonathan: "Dorothy was my landlady when I first came to Malvern and started house-hunting. She runs a small B&B now. She appears so quiet and gentle, but there's steel inside her."

"I can believe that, if she's a good friend of Charity's! Hey, what's the latest with this Midsummer madness?"

"We were just talking about that before you came!" said Emerald eagerly.

"Yes," added Feargal, "there've been more Vinegar Valentines sent to people. We're trying to find a connection."

"And we think that, *just maybe* ... there is none." This from Tamsin.

"None?" queried Jonathan.

"Yes - maybe the nasty person is scattering these cards about to mask the identity of the person they really want to upset," explained Feargal.

"Meanwhile upsetting a lot of other people."

"No-one's suggesting this person is operating with a full deck!" Emerald chipped in.

"And that makes it all the harder to identify him," sighed Charity.

"Or her," said Emerald. "They do say that poison pens are usually women."

"I think you may have been reading too much fiction!" teased Feargal. Then he said thoughtfully, "I wonder if I can find that out from ... from the cop shop."

"Tsst!" chorused Tamsin and Emerald, making mole noises. They liked nothing better than teasing Feargal about his mole in the police station.

"Actually," Charity interrupted this mirth, "I was looking at a book in the library the other day. It seems that blaming women for writing poison pen letters was more a reflection of the general scorn for women at the time, and has no basis in truth. In fact, most of these nasty letters are written by men."

"How very interesting," Tamsin chewed her lip thoughtfully.

"So Emerald's right, in that it could be either," said Jonathan. "So why do we tend to think it a male?"

"So far, all the cards have been sent to women, with very chauvinistic remarks in," Tamsin explained.

"That's not conclusive," said Feargal firmly, then filled his mouth with a large spoonful of the Furies' voluptuous carrot cake and turned his attention back to Emerald.

"So we're not any nearer?" asked Jonathan.

"Feargal thinks they're laying the ground for some kind of showdown - perhaps at the Midsummer Valentine."

"From what you tell me, that would be awful for Saffron!"

"It would indeed," agreed Tamsin. "And I, for one, intend to prevent it - though I've no idea how, just at the moment."

Noticing that Feargal and Emerald were now engaging Charity in conversation, Jonathan took the opportunity to speak quietly to Tamsin. "Fancy a dog walk this week?" he asked, hopefully. "We could walk on the Hills if you'd prefer that to an orchard this time round."

Tamsin smiled at him. "I'd love that. It'll be nice for my lot to see Teal again. How about meeting at the Beacon car park?" And they fixed a day and time.

Jonathan jumped up, saying, "Great! Lovely! See you then. Must dash back to rescue Manic .." and he was gone.

Charity turned to Tamsin. "That one, my dear," she said, nodding sagely, "is a keeper." And before Tamsin could protest she returned to her conversation with Emerald, who was looking unaccountably glad.

CHAPTER ELEVEN

It was on the following Monday that Charity and Tamsin could be seen strolling through the shadier parts of Great Malvern's Priory Park. The day was glorious - the bright June sunshine sparkling on the pond. Charity had her small brown fluffy Muffin with her, as ever, and Tamsin had brought her blue merle Border Collie Banjo. As dogs had to stay on lead in this park, it meant he could stay close to her and feel a bit safer, despite all the people and other dogs.

"How come there's this beautiful park right in the middle of town, Charity?" asked Tamsin, as she paused to take a photo looking up into the branches of one of the magnificent trees, of which there was a fine collection.

"Oh, it was the grounds of a big house originally. What is now the Malvern District Council offices."

"That extraordinary Victorian building that looks like a castellated manor house?"

"That's the one. This was its garden. It was designed at a time when it was all the rage to plant as many large exotic trees as possible."

"We should be very grateful to that rich townsperson."

Charity nodded and gazed up at the fine trees towering around them.

"When the Council bought it, they made the gardens into this park. And the new town swimming pool? That was the private pool of the old house."

Tamsin took a couple more pictures, of a Scots Pine, a huge Cedar of Lebanon, and a pretty bridge over the large pond, where a squirrel perched on a rock twitching its whiskers.

"And talking of the Council, there's that man I told you about .." Charity nodded towards the top of the path.

"Rex? Or Reginald?"

"Don't tease a poor old lady! It's Michael, as well you know. Now who's he talking to?"

"The guy with the grey pony tail? I can tell you that. It's Lucinda's new fella. Remember Lucinda, the artist?"

"I do ... they're looking very conspiratorial, don't you think?"

"They are! I think I want to get a bit closer." And so saying, Tamsin got her phone out of her pocket and trotted up the path with Banjo to study the big Oak there. Charity sighed, shook her head, and plonked herself down on a nearby bench to wait with Muffin.

By the time Tamsin came back, she was wearing a worried frown.

"What did you hear, dear?"

"Very odd. Lucinda's bloke - Jefferson, I just remembered his name, because it began with a Y," she grinned, "He passed Michael a large manila envelope, then said, 'I think we've done enough. It's plain sailing now.'"

"No! What could he be meaning? I mean the words are innocent enough. It could be anything .."

"Not the way he said them!" Tamsin sat down on the bench beside her. "He *hissed* them out."

"So what did Roger, I mean Michael, say to that?"

"This is the funny bit. He said, 'And we're only just getting started. The fun and games will soon begin!' You know, Lucinda is a good egg. What's she doing mixed up with this Jefferson fellow and his plotting?"

"Strange," said Charity, "Very strange. She is nice, I remember meeting her at your photography exhibition at The Cake Stop. Beautiful detailed plant drawings she does, doesn't she. I do hope this man isn't a rotter!" And she stroked Muffin's ears thoughtfully for a moment. "Now, dear, I know you want this to be about the Valentines. But really, it could be about anything!"

"You're right. It could. It's so frustrating, watching people get these cards and not being able to do anything about it. It's such a hateful thing to do. Some of them are deeply upset. I'm sure I would be too." She plucked a blade of grass from Banjo's mane. "And I do feel that they're leading up to something."

"It would be awful if there were a scene at Saffron's event. She's worked so hard to make something for herself and her little Charlie."

"Hey, talk of the devil! Isn't that Saffron over there by the stream? With a pushchair?"

"Oh, I think it is. She must have the afternoon off from the health shop. Let's go over and see her!"

As they approached, Saffron cried out, "Oh no Charlie! Oh Lord .." as young Charlie launched his bear into the water, pointed at it for a moment, then burst into loud howls as it began to submerge. "Not Fuzzy Bear!" wailed Saffron, as she lifted her skirt so she could kneel down at the water's edge.

"Hold on!" called Tamsin, running ahead of Charity with Banjo. We'll get that for you." And, pointing to the rapidly sinking bear, said, "Banjo, gettit!" Into the water sploshed the dog, and returned in seconds with a soaking wet, somewhat threadbare, Fuzzy Bear in his mouth. Tamsin took the bear, made sure Banjo's nose was facing her, said "Shake!" and watched the rainbows form in the showers of water that came off both sides of the dog.

Saffron scrambled to her feet and comforted her baby who had lost his precious bear. "Oh, thank you, Tamsin - how wonderful you and Banjo should appear at the right moment. I'm sure I'd have fallen in, reaching out for it. I just picked Charlie up from the minder, so Napoleon's still at home. But he'd have been useless anyway, I'm sure," she shrugged helplessly.

"I know how important these things are," laughed Tamsin. "It would be like Banjo here losing his beloved ball on a rope. Perhaps you could get to my tricks class some time? It would be very helpful if Napoleon could fetch the nappy basket, and pick up things that are dropped."

"I should! You're right." Saffron turned away and wrung the bear out over the stream. "Fuzzy will have to have a bath at home, Charlie, and when he's nice and dry you can have him back." She passed the back of her wet hand over her brow, smearing a black curl over her forehead, tucked the sodden and slightly green bear in the tray under the baby's seat, and lifted him out of the pushchair to comfort him.

"So how are things going with the Midsummer Valentine, my dear?" said Charity, who had caught them up and was making faces at Charlie to help stop his crying. Sure enough, a broad smile spread across his face and he rested his head on his mother's shoulder, pointing at Muffin and gurgling with delight.

Saffron returned him to the buggy, steering it away from the water's edge, and they all started walking together. "We've almost reached capacity with the sales," she said. "And apart from some hiccups with the caterers - you'd expect that, wouldn't you - it seems to be going well. They'll be erecting the marquee in Bill Lett's field on the twentieth, and I'll have all day on the twenty-first to get it ready," she chattered on. "Charlie will be going to his minder for the whole day and that night, won't you Charlie boy?" she looked fondly at her baby. "The caterers should be dealing with all the tables and whatnot. I hope I won't have too much to do."

"I think it's very enterprising of you, dear. I do hope it's a tremendous success," said Charity. "Are you planning on running more events?"

"I am, actually, yes! I think it's a way I can earn some decent money without having to commit to something full-time. I want to be at home for Charlie! I've learnt a lot so far about how to do it. And how not to do it!" she grinned. "But here," she pulled up short and turned to face Tamsin. "What happened with those nasty cards you mentioned? There haven't been any more, have there?"

"Actually, there have been a couple."

"That we know of," said Charity.

"Oh no! This has got to work!" Saffron frowned as she bit her lip anxiously.

"They're only sent to women, as far as we know, and they don't show any special knowledge of the person. Just general insults, nothing particular."

"It's all very nasty," Charity shook her head slowly.

"Just a sicko being unpleasant?" said Saffron hopefully.

"Hmm. Maybe. But whatever it is, we want to try and stop it - well before Midsummer Night."

"It's so good of you to help like this, Tamsin! I really appreciate it."

"I think she can't help herself," said Charity with a smile, "this crusader, this righter of wrongs. She just has to get involved."

"Well, please take care, Tamsin! I'd hate for anything to happen to you."

"Nothing's going to happen to me, don't you worry," said Tamsin with a toss of the head. "I'm going to whiz now," she added, peering up to the top end of the park. "There's something I want to do .. C'mon Banjo Bunny," And she was gone.

CHAPTER TWELVE

What had caught Tamsin's attention was the sight of Jefferson once more in conversation with another man - this time she couldn't see who it was, so she walked fast up the slope to catch up with them without appearing too obvious.

As she neared the two men, Jefferson turned and looked back down the path. Ducking behind the delicate tracery of the wrought iron Victorian bandstand she felt as if her ears were on stalks - like Banjo's erect ears as he looked up at her, wondering what on earth she was doing.

At first she could only hear mumbling. "Michael wants to .." she heard, from Jefferson.

Then another voice said, "So he does, does he?" followed by a big guffaw. She knew straight away who that was! It was Bill Lett, the farmer from Halfkey who had inflicted himself on her in The Pig and Sparrowgrass. What could these two be plotting? And where did Michael fit in?

There was more talk that she couldn't make out as the two men started to walk away. She crept out from behind the bandstand and strolled after them, stopping to study the foliage of a bush whenever they paused or looked as though they may turn round.

But they didn't, and before she knew it, she was on Orchard Road following them along the pavement beside the parked cars - one of which was her *Top Dogs* van. Both men got into a muddy old Land Rover - a farm workhorse that had definitely seen better days. As they motored away noisily, she hopped Banjo up into the back of the van, jumped in to the driver's seat and set off after them.

"Let's see what they're up to, Banjo Bunny," she said as she drove, her heart racing. Once they headed out of the town, the Land Rover driver put his foot down and she struggled to keep up with them, but managed to keep sight of the old jeep, taking a left, and another left. For a moment they had disappeared, then she saw the jeep coming back along the road towards her. As they passed, the occupants both stared at her.

She pulled up shortly after and thumped the steering wheel with her fists. "Cover your big pointy ears, Banjo, I'm going to swear!" And so she did.

They had clearly seen her and trapped her into following them in a circle. She felt a fool. "This isn't as easy as it seems on the telly," she said to her patient collie, as she did a three-point turn to head back home. "But then undercover policemen don't usually drive around in a white van with *Top Dogs* emblazoned on each side. It kinda gives the game away, don't you think?"

So it was a slightly dispirited Tamsin who arrived back at Pippin Lane. If anything could cheer her though, it would be a joyful greeting from Quiz and Moonbeam, and they didn't disappoint. Opal, of course, was disdainful as ever, standing on the worktop swishing her tail and glowering at her almost-empty food bowl.

Ignoring the cat's imperious demands, Tamsin got everything ready for her evening class in Nether Trotley, and once settled with a restorative coffee, she set about texting Feargal.

What links a farmer, a council employee, and a shady bloke?

His answer came back before her coffee was half-drunk:

Planning permission?

Tamsin pressed speed dial and rang him. After regaling him with what she'd seen and heard, and glossing lightly over the folly of her car-tailing, she asked, "Is this something you can easily delve into? Or should I?"

"I think me rather than you, old thing." Tamsin gritted her teeth, but let him continue. "Anyone who's applied for planning permission can watch their page for comments and progress. Now, it's possible that a council employee would be able to see who'd visited the page too. Not definite, but just possible. So you don't want to be doing it. I have ways and means .."

"You would have, you techno-geek, you!"

"Have to keep one step ahead," he laughed.

"So you can access the page secretly?"

"Sort of, yes. They wouldn't be able to trace me - without the most sophisticated software."

"I'll definitely leave you to it!" Tamsin sighed, "I really thought I was on to something - to do with the Valentines, I mean. But it seems we've discovered something else."

"It may be, it may be. I'll have a sniff round, ask a few questions. Is it this guy Michael you're talking about?"

"Yes, and Bill Lett, from Malvern Springs Farm, and Jefferson. Don't know any more about him. He's Lucinda the botanical artist's current squeeze."

"Unlikely trio, it's true."

"It's awfully coincidental that they're all involved with Saffron's event. And surely it's not them doing the nasty Valentines! Where would that fit in?"

"You're right. Maybe we have to look elsewhere for the small-minded person sending those cards."

Tamsin sighed. "We're back to the beginning. And there's only a couple of weeks to go!"

"Don't worry, kiddo. We'll crack it - we always do! While I'm looking into this planning permission, you have another look at those lists and see who could be doing it. And think about why. It may not be at all obvious. People have such strange motivations."

"It may not be what we think, you mean? Hmm. What *do* we think? I'm a bit baffled."

"Could be someone who gets his kicks from upsetting people. Or who's getting ready to do something very nasty. Or, who knows, maybe it's someone who has a warped sense of humour?"

"Someone with few scruples ... I'll take another look at that list. Let me know what you find!" She was about to ring off, then added, "Oh, and take great care of my friend Emerald, won't you."

"Without a doubt. You have my word," Feargal said earnestly. "I'd never do anything to hurt her. Never."

Taking that as the nearest thing to a declaration of love she was ever likely to hear from her reporter friend, she smiled as she ended the call.

CHAPTER THIRTEEN

On Tuesday morning Tamsin was determined to get to the bottom of the poison cards. But exhaustive study of the two guest lists hadn't got her any nearer, despite endlessly running her hands through her ever more tousled hair. So she decided to go into town and look for inspiration there.

"Your turn, Moonbeam!" she said, "Let's get you saddled up," and picking up her rose pink lead and harness she dressed her tiny dog, gave her a kiss on the end of her tiny black nose, and set off in the *Top Dogs* van.

Sure enough, it wasn't long before she gravitated towards The Cake Stop, and was delighted to see Lucinda sitting at one of the tables, clad in multi-coloured tie-dyed clothing with a bright orange shawl atop the lot, scribbling in a sketchbook.

"Hey there, Lucinda!" she said cheerily, carrying her mug of coffee. "May I join you? Or are you meeting someone?"

"No no! Come and sit down - haven't seen you for ages!" She put away her sketchbook. "How's the photography going?"

"You'll have to have a look at my *Top Dogs* website," she said, settling Moonbeam on her mat beside her chair. "It's had a complete rebrand, and loads of doggy pictures added. I really learnt a lot from the course. Did you? I mean, I know you're already an artist and know all about how to frame images and all that, but ..."

"Oh, I did. Such a funny fellow, that teacher Oliver, just like an owl! But yes, he helped me with focus - depth of field - and lighting on the close-up reference photos for my botanical drawings."

"I guess you need a huge amount of detail?"

"I do! The drawings have to be accurate or scientists and publishers wouldn't want them. So it's important to be sure there's no distortion - in size or shape."

"So why don't they just use a photograph themselves?"

"The artist can bring so much more to the image! The colour, the roots, the flowers - we can put buds, flowers, young and mature leaves all on the same drawing! We can remove the shadows so the colours are true. A photograph can't do that."

"The artist's eye makes sense of what they're seeing."

"Exactly! So we can show you what *you're* seeing. You might miss it otherwise."

Tamsin took a sip of coffee. "Hey, aren't you going to Saffron's Midsummer Valentine? I'm sure I saw your name on the guest list. I'm helping her a little, you see."

"I am! And I'm looking forward to it."

"I bet you'll turn up in some exotic evening garb," giggled Tamsin, nodding at Lucinda's arty colourful clothing.

"I just love vintage dresses - I've got a few," she grinned in reply.

"And what will your partner be wearing? It's Jefferson, isn't it? Will he wear hippie clothes too?"

Lucinda tossed the orange shawl across her shoulder. "I think he'll probably smarten up alright," she mused. "He's often involved in business meetings, I know."

"What does he do?" Tamsin tilted her head enquiringly, her eyes large. It was an innocent enough question, but seemed to stump Lucinda.

"Oh, er, he has, er, some business interests .." she tailed off lamely.

Tamsin decided to let this pass. "So how are you guys getting on? It's been a month or so now, hasn't it?"

Lucinda blushed slightly. "Five weeks. Surprisingly fast, actually."

"You're happy?"

Lucinda avoided answering this leading question by calling out "Charity! Come and join us!". Tamsin had had her back to the window so she hadn't seen her friend approaching.

But Moonbeam had! And there was a joyous amount of tail-wagging as Muffin hauled her diminutive owner across the room.

"Drop the lead, Charity - I'll catch her." And Charity did, weaving between the tables, greeting her public on the way, and arriving to find Muffin and Moonbeam lying happily on the mat together.

By the time Charity's tea arrived, and they'd pulled up another chair for her, Tamsin explained that they'd just been talking about the Midsummer Valentine, and what they were going to wear.

"You never told me what *you* are planning!" protested Lucinda.

"That's because I have no idea - it'll be a last-minute shop for me, on the day before Midsummer Eve. How about you, Charity? You're coming, aren't you?"

"Yes, dear. Dorothy and I will come together. We don't have escorts like you young things, but we can still enjoy ourselves," she smiled. "As long as we don't get one of those horrid cards, that is."

"Cards?" Lucinda looked baffled.

"Hadn't you heard, my dear? Some poor soul has been sending poison Valentines to people - it's most unfortunate. Have you got anywhere near identifying the miscreant, Tamsin?"

"Oh, how nasty!" said Lucinda, wrapping her shawl more tightly round her.

"It's hard to understand the motive," replied Tamsin obliquely. "Is it to destroy Saffron's event? Or just because they're bats in the belfry? Or is there someone in particular they're targeting?"

"A jealous woman, perhaps?" asked Lucinda.

"Actually, we think it's more likely to be a male."

Lucinda gulped and stayed quiet. Tamsin wondered what she was thinking. It seemed that she'd found that Wonderboy Jefferson had feet of clay from the way she'd abruptly changed the subject when Charity appeared. Maybe she was having doubts about him, realised she really didn't know him that well yet. And this made Tamsin think about what she'd seen and heard in Priory Park the day before. Her antennae were twitching!

"I'm going to love you and leave you," she drained her coffee, and stood up and picked up Moonbeam's mat after the two dogs jumped off it. "There's somewhere I need to be." And leaving a puzzled Charity and a slightly relieved Lucinda, she added, "Lovely to see you both," and left the café.

CHAPTER FOURTEEN

Tamsin drove up through the Wyche Cutting - barely pausing to enjoy the wonderful panorama spread out before her as she emerged on the western side - right round the Hills to the little village of West Malvern, and pulled up outside The Pig and Sparrowgrass.

As she got out of the van and inhaled the fresh, warm, morning air, she was glad to see no sign of the battered Land Rover, and hoped Bill Lett had already had his early morning snifter and was now - perhaps - actually doing some work on his farm.

Moonbeam trotted smartly beside her as she went through the low door, causing coos of delight from Marjorie as she spotted the little dog.

"Ooh, what a gorgeous little thing you are!" she said, bending her plump frame enough to reach down to Moonbeam. "My! What big ears you have!"

"All the better to hear you with!" laughed Tamsin. And after such an auspicious start, she ordered 'one of your lovely coffees' and perched on a bar stool, with Moonbeam on her lap.

"And how are you, my lovely?" asked Marjorie as she put the pottery mug in front of Tamsin.

"Well," Tamsin looked meaningfully round the pub, where there were a couple of old men playing dominoes, and three ladies knitting, "It's a bit quieter than last time I was here!"

"Oh, you mean that gert lummocks Bill Lett! Don't you mind him, my dear. He's a bit rough, but .."

".. doesn't mean any harm?"

Marjorie glanced about her, then said quietly, "I'm not so sure I'd go that far."

"What do you know, Marjorie?" Tamsin leant towards the bar, equally conspiratorially.

"Well, I do hear things, you know." She pulled herself up and folded her arms across her ample chest. Tamsin waited expectantly. "Like that time he was taking beasts to market and loaded up some of his neighbour's as well, to do him a good turn. Only the lots seemed to get muddled up and the unsold cattle he brought back to his neighbour didn't seem to be the same as those that went."

"Don't cattle all have paperwork these days?"

"I do believe they do, but back in the day if they weren't tagged, youngstock look much the same as each other."

"Ooh," said Tamsin encouragingly.

"It's a while now since they started this tagging lark," Marjorie conceded, then brightened up. "But I do know that that partickler farmer still won't speak to Bill Lett." She nodded emphatically, her double chins echoing the nod.

"He's a regular patron here, is he?"

"Oh that he is - likes his drink, does Bill." Marjorie nodded enthusiastically.

"Likes it a lot?" Tamsin was enjoying egging the barmaid on.

"I'd say so, yer. There's been times when I don't know how he's got home in that battered jeep of his."

"So .. is he a good farmer?"

"Nah. His farm is a dump. Don't know how he makes ends meet." Marjorie looked very obviously from side to side before leaning forward and saying in a stage whisper, "Wouldn't surprise me if he's got the measure of all these subsidies they can get."

Tamsin nodded. "A bit wide, altogether?"

Marjorie clearly thought she'd said too much. She shrugged, pursed her lips, and said, "Now don't let me keep you from your coffee, my duck. You don't want to let it get cold! I just has to check on this barrel." And she disappeared from the bar.

"Interesting, eh, Moonbeam?" Tamsin said softly to the little bat-eared dog on her lap. And - for once - she did as she was bidden, finished her coffee, and left the Pig and Sparrowgrass.

Once in the van and motoring homeward, she realised she couldn't do much more with these three men till Feargal came back to her. She certainly didn't want to visit a grotty, ill-kempt, farm, and she certainly couldn't go snooping round Jefferson after seeing Lucinda that morning.

So she decided to go home and take a fresh look at the two guest lists and see what she could come up with by taking a completely different angle. And that way she could spend some more time with all three of her dogs.

"Time I did some more tracking with Quiz," she said over her shoulder to Moonbeam as she motored down the eastern face of the Malvern Hills towards home. "Tell you what," she chattered on, "I'll stop at the paddock and lay a track now, then it'll be just an hour old by the time I've settled you back and had some lunch." Moonbeam said nothing, but cocked her ears prettily. "It's a warm dry day, so that'll make it harder," chuckled Tamsin, always ready to challenge her dogs gently by making things slightly harder, then easier, then harder again.

CHAPTER FIFTEEN

After Quiz had worked a stunningly successful half-mile track with seventeen turns, recovering all three tiny articles - a spark plug, half a wooden clothes peg, and a piece of knotted baler twine - Tamsin set off in her van with all three dogs. "You need a big reward for that brilliant track," she told Quiz as she drove. "We're going to meet Jonathan and your friend Teal!" The sides of the van were thumped noisily by Banjo and Quiz's tails. Tamsin had arranged to meet Jonathan at the Beacon car park, and she felt full of the joys of spring, humming to herself as she drove.

She'd only got as far as the junction to the top road when she spotted Bill Lett's tatty old jeep passing right in front of her. She would have ignored it, but she caught sight of Jefferson's grey pony tail, and on the spur of the moment decided to pull out and follow them.

Why?

She couldn't say. And later, she very much wished she hadn't.

They were heading towards Leigh Sinton - presumably going to Bill's farm, Malvern Springs. But she was itching to know what this unlikely pair were up to.

"We may be able to see something," she told the dogs, as she frowned at the back of the Land Rover and kept back a little, allowing another car to drive between them. Eventually, Bill turned off - predictably - at his farm, and Tamsin drove on past.

"Curse it! I've learned nothing. Am I getting rusty, dogs?"

The single tail-wag in reply, gently brushing the side of the van, was inconclusive.

"We're going to have fun now, though! We're going for a walk, and it's a beautiful June day!" and she let her thoughts wander round the pleasant prospect of an hour or two with Jonathan and Teal, and got a warm fuzzy feeling.

So warm and fuzzy that she didn't notice that now it was she who was being followed.

She drove back along the top road, through the Wyche Cutting, and up to the car park, unaccountably empty on such a lovely day. She was still a bit early, so she gazed out at the view across Herefordshire while she carried on with her warm, fuzzy thoughts.

Really Jonathan was turning out to be a bit of a find. He was kind, solicitous, liked dogs, he had a farm and a terrific cider business - and .. it seemed that he was falling for her ... She came back from her reverie with a jolt, as she realised she was leaving the safe territory of her reasonable and ordered existence and wandering into the realms of fantasy.

"Ok dogs, let's get ready!" She flung open the van door, jumped out, and gasped as a hand grabbed her arm and another hand closed over her mouth. It was the work of a moment for her to be bundled - kicking and making muffled squawks - into the waiting Land Rover to be driven away.

CHAPTER SIXTEEN

Jonathan drove his car up the bumpy approach to the Beacon car park, and felt a broad smile spreading over his face as he spotted the *Top Dogs* van. He pulled up the far side of it, got out of the car, ran a hand through his hair, straightened his shirt, and went round to the driver's side of the van.

No Tamsin.

From the front of the van he could see the dogs standing waiting in the back, their tails waving softly as they recognised him.

"Hey dogs! Where's your Mum?" he asked.

They couldn't tell him.

"Maybe she's answering a call of nature?" Jonathan waited for a couple of minutes by the van. "This is not like Tamsin .." he muttered. "She's always prompt." He frowned and started to pace up and down beside the van. His foot kicked against something which gave a metallic clink. He bent to see what it was, and scooped up a bunch of keys. Turning them over he saw a key fob bearing an image of Quiz, with *Top Dogs* written on it. He pressed the key button, and the van's lights flashed and the doors locked.

Jonathan's heart sank. This was not good. He unlocked the van again and opened the tailgate, which he knew had an inner cage door. The dogs' leads were all still hanging there. "It's ok dogs, we'll find her," he said to the patient dogs, though he had no idea how he was going to do it. The beauty of his surroundings - the fresh warm greenery, the spectacular view - were invisible to him as his heart tensed within him.

He breathed out and counted slowly to ten while he formulated a plan.

His first step was to call the police. He didn't know what kind of reception he'd get, reporting someone missing after only a matter of minutes, but he knew something was very wrong. It was his good fortune that the duty sergeant today was the one who'd had dealings with Tamsin over all the cases she'd been involved with, and who was willing to listen.

"Oh dear, what's she done now? Stay there, sir, and we'll get someone up to you."

Next, he rang Manic. "I need help," he began. "I'm meant to be meeting Tamsin in the Beacon car park. Her van is here with the dogs in, and she's not."

"That doesn't sound like Tamsin!" said Manic. "She never leaves those dogs alone for more than a few seconds."

"What's more, I found her keys on the ground by the van. It wasn't locked."

"She left the dogs in the van and didn't lock it?" Manic was aghast.

"Manic, I've got an awful feeling. I think she's been taken."

There was silence at the other end of the phone. "Have you told the police?"

"I have. They seem to be taking it seriously. They're sending someone over."

"Listen mate - stay there. I'll be there in ten."

And long before that, a Police Constable arrived in his blue and yellow car. Jonathan felt foolish as the PC asked him to step away from the driver's door of the van.

"Now, I know you've been standing here, sir, but do you see them marks there?"

Jonathan gasped. "I do! I never noticed them before."

"Takes training, it does," said the young PC, pulling himself up to his full height. "Them looks like scuff marks to me. In fact - look over here," he pointed to some more disturbed dust. "That's heelmarks, that is! Looks like your friend was dragged away over here .." He stepped to the centre of the track. "Guess she was put in a vehicle and taken away. That's your answer!" He beamed proudly, throwing his shoulders back and his chest out.

"No! That's not the answer - that's the *problem*." Jonathan snapped back. "The answer will be finding her!"

The Constable looked deflated. "Very hard to know where to look, sir. Do you know anyone as had it in for her, like?"

Jonathan frowned. "I haven't seen her for a few days. I know she was working on something ... I tell you what! I'll ring Feargal Wallis, he may know."

"Ah, that be the young reporter gentleman, am I right?" the PC nodded sagely.

Jonathan was already on the phone looking for Feargal, and fortunately for both his hair and his blood pressure, it didn't take long to find him.

And what he learnt chilled him to the marrow.

"She what?!" he exclaimed, as he pressed one hand over his ear so he could hear against the noise of Manic's bike approaching up the path.

As Manic pulled off his helmet and gloves, he strode up to his friend. "What's happening?" he asked.

Jonathan held the phone away from his ear. "Feargal's saying Tamsin had got wind of some planning permission scam involving people tied up with the Midsummer Valentine event. He thinks she may have tried to interfere!"

He turned back to the phone. "Yes, got that. Yes .. Yes .. Ok, I'll pass that on to the police here. They could make a start." He turned to the constable and gave him the names he'd just heard from Feargal. "Michael Cummings at the Council offices, Jefferson something, and Bill Lett. Got that?"

The PC nodded as he wrote the names down in his notebook. "I'll report in, sir, and get the wheels turning, don't you worry! I have to carry on my round in West Malvern, but they'll get it in hand down the station."

Manic spoke to Jonathan quietly. "You don't think she'd kind of wandered off for a bit?"

"I don't. But I could stay here for a bit longer in case. I've phoned her, of course, but her phone is ringing in the van. She doesn't have it with her."

"It's beginning to get hot," said Manic, glancing up through the tree branches at the cloudless blue sky. "Tell you what, give me those keys. I'll run the van down to her house and get the dogs indoors. Give me a few minutes to settle them and then you can come and get me so I can come back and collect my bike. Something may have happened by then."

Jonathan nodded dumbly. Manic clapped him on the shoulder. "We'll find her. We animal-lovers stick together." And he took the keys and his helmet and climbed into the van.

The police had gone, and now Manic and the dogs had gone too. Jonathan walked aimlessly about, crouching to see if he could find any more clues in the area. He picked up a stone and flung it viciously into the undergrowth. He'd never felt so wretched or so helpless.

"Come on Teal," he said to his dog as he climbed back into his car. "Sorry about the walk. Let's fetch Manic."

And he drove off the Beacon.

CHAPTER SEVENTEEN

"I don't care!" Emerald almost stamped her elegant foot as she turned moist eyes to Feargal. "I don't think Jonathan and Manic have slept. They've been hunting all night. Nothing." She buried her face in her hands and Feargal pulled her close.

"So you want to go hunting yourself, I understand," he soothed her.

"The dogs need to get out, and if anyone can find her, it's them!"

"The police have been to the addresses of the three men."

"But they don't have *evidence*, so they weren't able to force their way in and search! We can!"

"I see I'm not going to be able to dissuade you. Where do you want to start?"

"I think somewhere near that man's Farm. We can start at the field where the marquee is going to be. Say we're something to do with Saffron if we're asked."

"Hasn't Jonathan already been up there?"

"Yes, but he couldn't find anything, and it was dark. We've got secret weapons!" She looked down at the three anxious dogs.

"Ok. Let's get going. C'mon doggos - this is your moment."

They drove past the front entrance of Malvern Springs Farm and

Feargal peered in to the yard as they passed. "I don't see his jeep. Tamsin said he drives a scruffy Land Rover."

"Let's hope he's out," said Emerald, her fists clenched and her face paler than ever.

Parking in a lay-by right round the other side of the farm, they got the harnesses and leads onto the dogs. Feargal managed to get Moonbeam's back to front before Emerald helped him with a giggle. They climbed over the padlocked gate into the marquee field, the dogs scrambling underneath. Feargal took Quiz's lead while Emerald hung on to the handles of Banjo and Moonbeam's.

The grass was short and pale here, as the hay had not long been taken off it. Keeping to the hedge to begin with, the dogs sniffed and snuffled. Banjo alerted to something in the ditch, behind the long grass. Emerald suddenly started to cry.

"What?!" hissed Feargal as he ran over to join her.

"Banjo's a cadaver search dog! I'm terrified of what he may find." Emerald's teeth were now chattering.

Feargal took her hand and led her away. "Look, it was just a moorhen," he said, as a little bird scuttled out of the long grass and leapt into the water with a plop. "Let's keep our heads."

Emerald gulped. "Ok. No more frights. This is a job. We'll do it right." And on they walked. It took them over half an hour to cover the whole field, and at last they climbed over and under the next gate, finding themselves in a field with overgrown hedges.

"I don't see anything," whispered Emerald.

"The grass is too dry to show tyre-tracks," Feargal began, then his arm was pulled out straight by Quiz, who had suddenly stiffened and was pulling hard into her harness.

"Follow her!" cried Emerald. "Tamsin says you should always trust your dog when they're tracking," and she ran behind Feargal as he was pulled along the side of the hedge by Quiz.

"Banjo's got it too!" Feargal called over his shoulder as he saw the blue merle collie, head down, right behind his heel.

Suddenly Quiz threw herself down on the ground, her nose close to something between her paws.

Banjo pulled forward and swished his tail with enthusiasm, as Feargal leaned over Quiz.

"It's a whistle! Is it hers?" he asked urgently, holding it up.

"Could be - she has loads of them. Quiz seems to think so, anyway. Good girl, Quiz! Let's keep going!" said Emerald breathlessly, her thumping heart preventing her breathing properly. Feargal pocketed the whistle.

They kept walking fast, the dogs still pulling firmly ahead of them.

"What's that?" whispered Feargal, pointing to a dark shape almost concealed in the straggly hedge.

"It looks like a kennel or something." Emerald hung on tight to Banjo's lead as he surged forward. By the time they reached the shed, both Quiz and Banjo snuffled and scrabbled at the door. "Open it!" squealed Emerald.

"There's a big padlock. Tamsin!" called Feargal, "Are you in there?"

They listened intently and heard a low moan.

Feargal looked at the rusty old hinges on the door. "Hinges look weak, stand back!" And he thumped first with his shoulder, then with his boot, at the door. It creaked but remained firm. Finally he leapt in the air and threw all his weight at it, and sure enough, the rotten wood under the hinges gave way with a ripping sound. He grabbed the edge of the door and pulled hard. Three dogs dived past him and in the gloom all Feargal and Emerald could see were waving tails and bouncing dogs on top of a prostrate Tamsin, her hands tied behind her back, and the remains of some tape on her face.

Feargal pulled out his pen-knife from a back pocket and cut the tape holding Tamsin's wrists, as Emerald carefully peeled the tape off her face, then gave her a huge hug, unable to speak with the tears streaming down her face.

They helped Tamsin up into a sitting position, and after rubbing her arms for a moment she wrapped them round her dogs, clasped a hand of each of her rescuers, then said through her tears, "Boy, am I hungry!"

CHAPTER EIGHTEEN

It took them twenty minutes to get back through the fields and over the gates. Tamsin was stiff and weak and clung on to Feargal all the way, struggling to scramble over the five-bar gates she could normally swing over with ease. Once they were all safely in the car and driving away - Tamsin lying on the back seat cuddling three very happy dogs - they could breathe more easily and in no time they were back at Pippin Lane.

"You need some food, girl," said Feargal as he helped her in, almost tripping over the jubilant dogs flying around. Opal stood on the worktop flicking her bushy tail and miaowed loudly, quite unconcerned with all the drama, but clearly pleased that her staff had returned.

"First things first. A bath." Tamsin said firmly, looking down meaningfully at her damp and smelly clothes. Emerald ran upstairs and started to run the bath, then looked out some clean clothes and laid them on Tamsin's bed. Feargal helped her up the stairs, and Emerald gently removed the foul clothing and held her friend while she stepped into the bath. She washed her hair and sponged her back, taking care round the bruises, while Tamsin soaped her hands and washed everything else, tilting her face back when Emerald used the shower to rinse her hair so that the warm water should wash away her tear stains.

By the time a considerably cleaner and fresher dog trainer descended the stairs, Feargal had the coffee ready, along with a lump of cheese and some bread, which reflected the extent of his meal preparation abilities. "Lie down on the sofa," he said, as he picked up the tray. "Jonathan and Manic will be here in a minute. I'm nearly deaf from the shriek Jonathan let out when I told him!"

And by the time they arrived, Tamsin was on her second mug of coffee, with only a few crumbs remaining on her plate. She lay on the sofa with Moonbeam tucked up close to her, and the opportunist Opal lying on her hip, purring.

"What do you look like?" she laughed as the two men came in, their clothes almost as scruffy as hers had been, and their faces dirty and unshaven.

Jonathan leaned over her and kissed her warmly. "You've led us quite a dance," he said, then turned to Manic who was carrying a large box. "But we know you, so we stopped off at The Cake Stop and bought this."

Manic lowered the box and opened the lid, to show a whole, magnificent, mango cheesecake.

Tamsin pushed herself up into a sit, and said, "Where's my plate?"

CHAPTER NINETEEN

By the time the cake had been polished off, by four very hungry searchers and their "starving" rescued friend, Tamsin was lying back on the sofa again, her legs across Jonathan's lap as he sat beside her, and Moonbeam lying against her tummy. Emerald bent over Tamsin to put more cream - something with beeswax and aloe vera in - on her sore cheeks and chin, still slightly red and blotchy.

"It looks as though you could do with a night's sleep," said Feargal, watching her.

"I sure could too!" said Jonathan, and Manic nodded in agreement.

Tamsin pushed herself up on her elbow. "I'll sleep well tonight - back in my own bed! But right now, I want to know what on earth is going on. I know it was Bill Lett and that creepy Jefferson who kidnapped me. But why?"

"I think I can help here," said Feargal, putting down his coffee mug and reaching for his trusty notebook.

"I'm all ears!" said Tamsin, as she stroked Quiz's head, which was resting on the sofa seat, her big brown eyes fixed on her beloved owner.

"Same here!" said Emerald. "What *is* going on?"

"I've been doing some sniffing about. And you're right, Tamsin.

There's something very unsavoury going on between those three. And my guess is that they saw you following them that time, and again yesterday, from what you were saying. They may have learnt that you've been asking questions ... Then Michael saw a lot of anonymous activity on the planning website - which was me - and they put two and two together .."

".. and made five," said Manic, with a tut.

"Exactly. You see, their planning application times out tomorrow. They must have thought you were about to spill the beans, and just needed to keep you quiet till after it had gone through."

"But what was I meant to be being quiet about?" protested Tamsin, lying back against her pillow again.

"I have an idea, but I'm not yet sure. A company called *Botanical Solutions* has put in for planning permission for a commercial solar panel array. They've named the location as Malvern Springs Farm. According to the maps they've submitted, it will be huge."

"But that's a good thing, isn't it?" said Emerald with a frown. "Solar energy, saving the planet ...?"

"It *would* be a good thing, if it happened. I've been talking to some of my colleagues in the business. It seems that the government subsidies for this kind of venture are massive. These three could stand to get hundreds of thousands between them."

"But won't they be spending a lot themselves as well?" Jonathan asked, reasonably. "I'm looking into getting solar panels on my barn rooves, and there's a big investment, even with any grants."

"They would, if it weren't a scam." Feargal leaned forward, his elbows on his knees. "Michael in the Council offices is making sure the planning permission goes through without a hitch. Then the company starts work at Bill Lett's farm."

"And who is this company, pray?" asked Jonathan.

Feargal raised an eyebrow. "Good question! *Botanical Solutions* happens to be the website of a botanical artist - one Lucinda Fry."

"No!" exclaimed Tamsin. "I don't believe Lucinda is involved in this! She's a good person. She's devoted to her art - those beautiful drawings she does .."

"You're probably right. But one of the directors of the company is Jefferson Smyth. The one who's been cosying up to her of late." Feargal leant back and crossed his legs. "So we have a company run by Jefferson putting in for planning permission for a large and expensive project with huge profits possible."

"We have this Michael guy in the Council, fast-tracking the application," said Manic, nodding, beginning to understand it all.

"And we have Bill Lett providing the land for the proposed project," said Emerald.

Tamsin gritted her teeth. "I knew I didn't like him, the minute I met him."

"Sorry, but how do they make all this money?" asked Emerald, half-hiding behind the large fluffy cream cat on her lap, afraid she was looking foolish.

"I don't get it either," said Manic, keen to ease Emerald's discomfort.

Feargal turned to her and explained, "They get it all approved. Then they apply for the massive grants, then - they falsify all the evidence. They just erect a handful of solar panels, and run into 'building issues' or something. They may have to 'buy' a bent official from the energy department concerned, but they'll have plenty of money to do that with."

"Enough to buy Farmer Lett any number of new Land Rovers!" said Tamsin, frowning.

"And enough for him to pack in farming and take early retirement," agreed Jonathan.

"Jefferson and Michael may be considering spending the rest of their days in the Caribbean, or South America ..." Feargal continued.

"And I bet he wouldn't be taking Lucinda with him," snorted Tamsin.

"It'd be more money than they'd ever seen in their miserable lives." Feargal reached for his coffee mug.

"And you," said Jonathan inclining his head to Tamsin, now looking very dozy on the couch, "and your inquisitive mind have rumbled this." He turned to Feargal. "How are we going to stop their beastly plan going through?"

"I think enlisting the help of the police for the possible scam would be a good start. Michael is quite high up in the planning department, so it needs to come from above him. I've already drafted a piece for the *Malvern Mercury* exposing them all."

"Oh wow!" said Emerald, "Your Editor will love that!"

"Especially with the suggestion of a kidnapping thrown in!" Manic chuckled.

"I hope so," Feargal beamed back at Emerald. "It's with the lawyers at the moment, but should come out later today, which means the police will have to look into it. We'll hand everything we have over to them so they can make a start by raiding the farm."

"And the first thing would be to block the application," Manic nodded. "Fair play to you, Feargal!"

"Ah," said Tamsin sleepily, "There are no spots on this tiger .."

"Bed for you," said Jonathan firmly. "You're rambling. Let's get you upstairs and Emerald can help you into bed."

"I think I meant 'no flies on Feargal'," she protested. "But," she sat up and opened her eyes fully, "we still haven't solved the poison Valentines! Saffron's event could still be wrecked - and where will she hold it if we hand Bill Lett over to the police?"

CHAPTER TWENTY

"That's a point," said Emerald. "He's hardly going to want to carry on with letting his field. He has bigger fish to fry."

"Why not?" asked Feargal. "He'll be under investigation, but not under arrest. He may be desperate for Saffron's money. And desperate to give a good impression too. Let's wait and see."

"We'll think of something," said Jonathan. "I'd help if I could. But I don't have any fields that aren't peppered with trees - apart from a small paddock, and it would take a lot longer than two weeks to get my spare barn cleaned up and ready!"

Manic, who was happily stroking Banjo's head - something that always made Tamsin smile, as her shy dog clearly accepted him as a friend - said, "We'll know in a couple of days - once that piece of yours is out. Saffron can talk to him then."

"There's something else we haven't discussed," Jonathan patted Tamsin's knees, still draped over his. "The kidnapping. You told the police we'd found her, did you not, Feargal?"

"I did. They said they'd go up and photograph the scene. Fortunately, being a reporter, I had the presence of mind to take some pictures while

Emerald was cleaning the mud off Tamsin's face. I've already sent those over to them."

Jonathan winced. "The place will be thick with blue and yellow cars by now, I hope."

"I hope they don't run over my whistle!"

"No worries - I have it here," and Feargal fished in his pocket and pulled out the whistle and handed it to her. "You knew you'd dropped it?"

"I felt it trying to escape from my pocket as they dragged me to that hut, so I wiggled a bit in the hope it would fall out. Who found it?"

"Quiz!" said Emerald with a smile.

"Bless you, Quizzy," and Tamsin bent to give her dog a kiss on the top of her nose.

Jonathan turned to Tamsin. "How did you get that tape off your face?"

"It wasn't as hard as I feared. Fortunately, I'd put on sun cream before our planned walk - it was such a lovely day - so the tape didn't stick very well. Then I kept rubbing my face on the earth floor. Once I'd got a corner lifted I was able to lick it and stretch my face .. Actually, I'd rather not think about it any more, if you don't mind. It makes me feel a bit sick .."

"Will I sleep in your room tonight, Tamsin?" asked Emerald. "I don't want to think of you having nightmares!"

"Thanks, Em. But the dogs should be sufficient company, I hope." She gave her friend a brave smile.

Jonathan stuck to his subject. "What's the punishment for kidnapping?"

Feargal answered straight away. "The minimum seems to be eight years."

"Bill Lett and the scummy Jefferson would be locked up for eight years?" echoed Tamsin.

"What about Michael?" said Manic.

Feargal paused. "Well, he wasn't directly involved in the kidnap - unless they find some incriminating evidence. For fraud he'd be looking at at least five years inside. And he'd never work in any official capacity again."

There was silence for a moment while they all chewed this over.

"I'd have to go to court," said Tamsin blankly. "I don't know if I could bear that."

Emerald reached out to hold her hand.

Jonathan said quietly, "Perhaps unmasking them in the *Mercury* as fraudsters would be enough. They'd presumably have to do time for that?"

"I would think so. The sums involved are potentially so large. The government doesn't take kindly to green energy fraud."

Tamsin leant back against her cushion. "That would be better, I think. As long as they're caught." Then she sat up again, "But what about the cards?"

Jonathan stood up. "Definitely past your bedtime," he said firmly, reaching to lift Tamsin off the sofa.

"No no, I can do this," she said, pushing away his hands, standing, then wobbling and falling weakly back on to the sofa.

"Come on you," said Jonathan, and they all got up and helped him negotiate dogs and cats and doors and other hazards as he carried Tamsin upstairs and deposited her on her bed. "I'll be round tomorrow, ok?" he said, giving her a kiss on her forehead.

And the men all left the house, leaving Emerald to play lady's maid.

As Tamsin climbed between the sheets, she laid back and let out a loud sigh.

The next thing she knew it was Friday morning, Quiz's tail was thumping the radiator, and Moonbeam was snuggled close up against her.

She woke blearily, wondering why parts of her felt so stiff and sore, then the reality of what had happened the day before hit her. She slumped back into her pillow, but there were two things she couldn't ignore - one was Quiz's thumping tail causing the radiator to go bong-bong-bong, and the other was the delicious aroma of coffee and, what was that? Pancakes?

She scrambled out of bed with a few 'ouch's' and 'oohs' and went down the stairs gingerly to let the dogs out. "Emerald?" she said, as she heard a sound and looked towards the kitchen.

"Emerald had to go out, dear, but she didn't want you to be alone, so I've come to make you breakfast!"

"Charity! What a delight you are!"

"She's told me *all* about it. So I'm to make sure you rest and recover - and feel properly looked after. I really wonder if you didn't go just a teeny bit too far, this time, dear?" Charity raised a quizzical eyebrow, drawing herself up to her full - albeit very short - height.

"Oh Charity. I'm beginning to think you may be right. But hey, where's Muffin? I have to let this lot out right now .." And she headed for the back door where her dogs - having thoroughly greeted their surprise visitor - were waiting to get to the garden.

"She's in the car," Charity told her as she came over to the kitchen counter. "I didn't like to bring her in till you were up. I did leave the windows open a bit, but the day is beginning to warm up."

"Go and get her now. Moonbeam will be delighted to see her! Though I expect Opal will make herself scarce," she nodded to the cream cat luxuriating in a patch of sunlight on the dining table.

"I don't think she'll need to. Muffin is very respectful of cats, ever since Sapphire made her nose bleed as a puppy when she first arrived. I'll go and fetch her now!"

Indeed there was a joyful meeting when the dogs came back in from the garden and Moonbeam saw her friend Muffin.

"You're right, Charity, it's a lovely day. I'll leave the garden door open - off you go, you two, you can chase around out there."

"I thought you may like your breakfast outside too?"

"That'll be nice! I'll throw some oats and fruit together while you finish those delicious-smelling pancakes, Charity. You have to eat something too!"

Tamsin carried the laden tray out to the garden and set it on the picnic table, shooing both the little dogs off it first. She gazed up at the Hills, now shimmering in the late morning sunshine, watched a couple of walkers - tiny figures silhouetted against the sky - heading up the Worcestershire Beacon, and sighed with satisfaction. She said to Charity, "No work till Puppy Class this afternoon. I could take the dogs out .."

"I really think they're getting plenty of stimulation here - look at them all, sniffing, playing, lolling about. They can do without a walk today while you rest."

"They did work hard yesterday, it's true. Charity, you've sold me on the idea. What could be better than sitting in the sunshine with a friend and four dogs, drinking proper coffee and eating good food?"

CHAPTER TWENTY-ONE

Tamsin managed to remain calm and soothed for exactly one hour. Then she turned to Charity and said, "We've collared three ne'er-do-wells for fraud. That's a major achievement. But we still haven't got to the bottom of the nasty cards."

"The fraud business is now in the hands of the police - with input from the *Malvern Mercury* I gather. So I'm glad you're well out of that. Those unscrupulous men are clearly dangerous. As for the cards .. They do seem to have slowed down. At least, I haven't heard of any new ones. Have you?"

"I've lost a day of my life. So I'm a bit out of touch. But no, you're right, I don't believe there have been any more. But that doesn't mean there won't be!"

"From what Saffron was saying the other day, it hasn't put people off. I mean, they're all still coming to the event."

"That's true. But supposing the nutcase has some awful plan for the evening? I really would like to get him or her under wraps before then. Saffron does deserve a break."

"She does. She may seem scatterbrained, but her heart is definitely in the right place, and she dotes on that baby of hers."

"Time for more coffee!" Tamsin jumped up with new-found energy - said "ouch!' and paused to rub her ribcage - causing all four dogs to watch for action. The two big dogs were lying in the shade of an ash tree keeping cool, the two small ones under the picnic table on the cool grass. Opal had by now transferred her dozing to the picnic table which was in full sunlight, the shade of the young ash tree having moved round, and she didn't twitch so much as a whisker.

"May I have tea?"

"Of course. I'll make both. And when I come out, we'll have thought of a solution to this card business," she grinned, and carried the tray back into the house, Quiz and Banjo following her.

While she went through the mechanical motions of making their pots of tea and coffee and washing the mugs, Tamsin thought hard. Stopping and relaxing was a good idea after all, she reflected, despite it being for a bad reason. She was really rather enjoying this enforced day off! So when she emerged into the sunshine again with the fresh tray of drinks, she felt lively - and curious.

"Well, Charity? What have you thought?"

"Oh thank you, dear," she responded, as Tamsin poured her tea. "I'm beginning to think it's more of a prank."

"Really? Why so?"

"I think if this were a genuinely mad or fixated person, who was trying to get at someone in particular - or just lashing out wildly at everyone - they'd be sending out *more* cards, not fewer."

"Hmm," said Tamsin, sipping her coffee and relishing it. "That's a point. It has gone a bit quiet."

"On the other hand," Charity began.

"Uh-oh!"

"On the other hand, they could be keeping their powder dry, ready for a big happening at the Midsummer Valentine."

"That's no help, Charity! As far as I can see, all we can do is keep watching out, and seeing if we can find a pattern in what the cards say, and who's been chosen to get them."

"I'm afraid that's true. Unless the police come up with something, we're powerless. But I think they're so busy with serious crimes that it's rather far down their list of priorities. If only I could think of someone who's attending this event who could have done it. I'll keep thinking."

"Have you got some ancient memory to draw on? So much seems to have happened in your life, Charity!"

"Well, I was remembering a boy called Jack Knight. He wrote a load of anonymous letters to teachers and children at school. They were easily traced to him - he wasn't the brightest, bless him."

"And why did he do it?"

"Turns out he was beaten at home. It was a way he could try and control others. He knew when he'd sent a letter and he could see the effect it had when it arrived. It gave him a tiny bit of power in his power-less world."

"How awful! Poor boy. Did he get into big trouble?"

"He didn't, no. It was handled pretty well - for the time. We had a very wise old Rector who took the boy under his wing. Gave him special tasks to do, so he could learn to take pride in what he did. He learnt that giving people pleasure was much more rewarding than being nasty to them. Even the children were kind to him when he pulled down his long socks and showed where he'd been whipped on the back of his legs."

"Poor child." Tamsin frowned and shook her head slowly. "So maybe our card person is just working off some hatred, directing it in the wrong place, so he can feel in control."

"And it's not personal at all. Yes, that may be so. In that case, I can't imagine them making a big hullabaloo on the night. That wouldn't fit in."

"You know what, Charity? I'm going to relieve you of your caretaker duties. I need to start preparing for Puppy Class, and I'm sure Emerald will be back from her yoga trainings shortly. It's been lovely having you here. You've really helped me slow down and count my blessings."

"Ah, my dear! If only you knew how many blessings you had to count!"

Tamsin glanced across at her quickly, but realised this enigmatic statement was not going to be elaborated on. She had to make do with a big hug from the thin old lady as she called Muffin and left Pippin Lane, with firm instructions to Tamsin that she had had a shock and was not to overdo it.

CHAPTER TWENTY-TWO

The Friday afternoon Puppy Class in Malvern was Tamsin's favourite class of the week, and when the people started to arrive she was delighted to see how some of them had grasped what she taught and already had a nicely-behaved, happy puppy, without any shouting or lead-yanking.

The class whizzed by quickly, as she taught the students strategies for managing dog walks, and checked that all the puppies were sleeping all night and the housetraining was going well. And yet, by the end of class she found herself feeling really tired again.

'Must be delayed shock or something,' she muttered to herself as she packed up her things, stacked the chairs, and started to clean the hall.

Mary had gone out to put Pedro in the car, and now she popped her head round the door. "Tamsin, you look a bit tired. Let me help you," and so saying, she took the broom out of Tamsin's hand and carried on the sweeping. In no time it was done, and she reached out to take one of Tamsin's bags as they headed out to the car park.

"Thank you so much, Mary - you're right, I am tired today. I hope that didn't show in the class?"

"Not at all - the class was great. But we have to look after you, dear! You're important. And you do important things."

Tamsin smiled at her, wondering if Mary would spot her slightly wobbling lower lip. "I'll see you next week, Mary," she said as she climbed into her van - and then it'll be time for the Midsummer Valentine! I'll meet Ernest too," she grinned, as she shut the door and put the van into gear.

She hadn't taken a dog with her to class this week - she had realised she simply didn't have the energy. So she arrived home and took all three of her precious dogs out for a walk where they could have a good bit of free running. She watched them as they ran and bounced - she enjoyed their beauty and sense of fun. So she felt somewhat restored when she came back home with them, though she did wonder why the walk home seemed so much longer today.

By the time she got back again, Emerald was home, and took up where Charity had left off, fussing over Tamsin.

"Just for once," said Emerald, trying to look authoritative, "you can take it easy and let someone else help you."

Now lying on the sofa under a duvet, Tamsin asked, "Am I really that difficult?"

"Well," Emerald softened and perched on the edge of the sofa. "You can take independence a bit far - sometimes!" she added quickly.

"That's the second odd thing someone's told me today."

"Charity been telling you home truths?"

"Hinting at them."

"I think we're all wondering how long it will take for you to see .." Emerald stopped herself.

"See what?"

"Oh," Emerald waved her beautiful hand airily, "just how much you mean to people, I suppose."

"Talking of meaning things to people," Tamsin half-sat, leaning on her elbow, anxious to move the subject away from her. "How's the planning going for your trip to France?"

"*Touché!*" Emerald smiled, then paused while she thought. "Feargal's so different from the sort of person I thought I'd like."

"He's different, alright. Part human, part Ferrari, I'd say."

"His energy is contagious, it's true."

"You know what? You're a match made in Heaven. He'll keep your feet on the ground, and you'll make sure he never becomes a sleazy reporter. You bolster his integrity."

Emerald's cheeks went a delightful shade of soft pink. She tossed her long blonde hair back and said, "Time for a zizz for you, Madam. Would you like a coffee to go to sleep with? I know it seems to have no effect on your ability to sleep!"

"That sounds wonderful!" Tamsin snuggled down under the duvet, now weighted down by a cat and a small dog.

And when Emerald came back in with the coffee, she found her friend fast asleep.

CHAPTER TWENTY-THREE

Tamsin awoke to the sounds of voices. She stretched, dislodging Opal, and realised she felt a lot better. Running her fingers through her hair, she sat up, cast off the duvet, and ambled in to the kitchen, three dogs padding along at her heels.

Feargal had arrived and was talking to Emerald. "Ah, the ghost of Christmas Past!" he said.

"I look that bad?"

"No no," said Emerald hastily, "just a little pale. Did you have a good sleep?"

"I did thanks, Nurse Emerald! What's the time?"

"Just gone seven," Feargal flipped his phone back in his pocket.

"Wow, I slept for hours. And you know what?"

"You're hungry!" chorused Feargal and Emerald together, and turned to look at each other in pleasant surprise.

Then Feargal said, "We know you, Tamsin! But fear not, Jonathan has texted me - your phone was off."

"Was it?"

"Sorry, that was me," Emerald admitted. "When I brought in your coffee and found you snoring, I switched it off. You needed to rest."

"Oka-a-ay. So .. what did Jonathan have to say?"

"He's coming round in about half an hour," said Feargal. "And you'll be glad to know he wanted to know how many to bring curry for! I told him to go to that new place on the way in to town."

"Ooh, lovely!" Tamsin looked lost for a moment, looking about her. "I think I'll go up and have a wash before supper," and she scampered up the stairs, with a new-found energy.

Jonathan was solicitous when he arrived, pleased to see that Tamsin's appetite was unaffected by her ordeal as they all ploughed through their massive curries - except for Emerald with her bird-like appetite. "Feargal tells me the police have been all over Malvern Springs Farm," he said.

"They have. And they've found the place where Tamsin was imprisoned - where I took the picture of. The good news is the council have put a hold on the application. There'll be no further consideration of it till the police have reported their findings."

"Things have been happening while I was dead to the world!" Tamsin was leaning back in her armchair, feeling comfortably full. "It's only a week now to Saffron's event. There've been no more cards, right?"

"So far as we know," said Feargal. "Perhaps you can stop worrying now?"

Tamsin sat up. "I won't rest till I've found out who did it!"

"It offends your sense of decency," declared Jonathan.

"It does. And - oh, I know it's not a big thing. Not like one of the murders we've been tangled up in before, but it smarts that I can't get to the bottom of it."

"I'm not sure you should carry on with these investigations at all," Jonathan said firmly. "This one turned very nasty, very fast!"

"I love what I do for a living - helping people to make their dogs' and their own lives happier - but I do like to get my teeth into something too!"

Jonathan leaned forward, "Then I have an idea for you - a project, if you like."

Tamsin looked at him, and for once looked right into his eyes.

"I've got an old barn that is only used for storage at the moment. It's at the other end of the farm, by the paddock. I think - if you could put your mind to it - you could make that a great base for *Top Dogs!*"

Tamsin's eyes widened. "Really? A building? And a field?" She looked from one friend to the other, and said, very quietly, pointing at her chest, "For me?"

"That's the idea," Jonathan sat back in his chair again, and smiled softly.

For once in her life, Tamsin was lost for words. "Oh wow," was all she could say, over and over again. "Oh wow."

After a period of uncharacteristic silence, Emerald said, "I can see you're making plans already in your mind! What have you dreamt up so far?"

"Well, I could start agility and hoopers sessions," Tamsin spoke quickly. "I'd have plenty of room to work on tracking and searching .. then classes could be in the barn, under cover .. We could even have the Christmas fancy dress party there!" Tamsin became more and more animated as the ideas popped into her head. "I could teach assistance dog work - you know, for alerting deaf owners to sounds, or picking things up for people who can't."

"Banjo's always picking things up for me!" said Emerald. "I deliberately drop things for him - he so loves it."

"And I could look into doing Dog Dancing - Heelwork to Music they call it - I've done a bit of that with Quiz ..."

Jonathan, smiling sphinx-like, was leaning back in his chair as Tamsin carried on excitedly generating ideas for a new phase in her business.

"Jonathan, is this for real?" Tamsin blurted out. "Really? A building and a field? Just for me?"

"Really," he carried on smiling like the cat that got the cream.

Suddenly her face fell. "But what about the rent? How much would it be? Oh dear, I didn't think .."

"No rent," said Jonathan, and Feargal suddenly turned to Emerald and said, "I nearly forgot! I got an email about the train tickets to the Pyrenees - here, come out to the kitchen and I'll show you," and he took

Emerald's hand and pulled her up, unceremoniously herding her through the door, which he carefully closed behind them.

"No rent," Jonathan said again into the quietness of the room. "Try it. I'd love you to. We can look again later. I'd like to help you make the most of your dog training business .. and," he added as he moved over to sit next to her on the sofa, "it just may keep you out of trouble." He put his hand over hers and she leant her head against his shoulder.

"We may not always be there to rescue you," he said, as he tilted her chin up and gave her a kiss.

CHAPTER TWENTY-FOUR

Tamsin spent several days on Cloud Nine, fantasising about her huge new dog training school. She was forever scribbling down notes as new ideas hit her. She was thinking of the students who came to her classes to shadow her and learn from her, and which of these she could train up to start taking some classes for her. She wondered if Mark Bendick's mother, Shirley, would enjoy doing the admin - or perhaps Yvonne of the Dachshunds ... Her mind whirred with ideas, what she'd need, how she'd manage it all, where to start and what order to do things in.

But she hadn't entirely put the poison Valentines out of her mind, and she was still doing her best to make the Midsummer Valentine a success. Saffron was getting nervous as the time grew closer, so she'd promised to do some more publicity for her, while hoping against hope that she'd have a shaft of light over who was doing this. She was so anxious to put it to bed before the event.

Still turning these thoughts over in her mind, and narrowing down the possibilities from the guest list she endlessly kept studying, of people with no scruples and a warped sense of humour, Tamsin dropped in to *Flying Pedals,* the main bike shop for the town, to leave some more flyers for Saffron. The bell jangled as she opened the door, alerting the figure stooped behind the counter adjusting a bike brake.

"Hi there, stranger!" came the cheery voice of Mark, the young lad who was making good, and who owed a debt of gratitude to Tamsin for helping him out of some previous scrapes. "Come to make my day and buy a bike?" he grinned at Moonbeam who hopped up into Tamsin's arms as she stood at the counter.

"My cycling days are well over!" she replied, as she fished some flyers out of her bag. "I can't fit three dogs in the basket, I'm afraid."

Mark chuckled obligingly.

"You doing ok, Mark?"

"I am, thanks for asking. Reckon my old life is behind me now." He smiled bravely.

Really he's just a big kid, Tamsin thought, but said, "Bet your Mum is a lot happier?"

"Oh, she is. And living with her and that gert big dog Luke is a sight better than being in the nick."

"I bet it is! Ok, can you pin up one of these flyers for me, and perhaps leave the rest on the counter for people to take? It's only a a few days away now."

"Right you be," said Mark, his big fist taking the flyers from Tamsin. "I'll find a pin later for this one," he said, waving the bigger sheet in the air.

The bell on the shop door jangled, and in swaggered a tall fair-headed young man.

"Wotcher, Johnny!" said Mark, "What can I do you for today?"

"I see you have company, Mark," the young man replied, plunging his hands into his jeans pockets and puffing out his chest. "It's our intrepid detective, is it not?"

"Now Johnny, you should know better than to taunt me. Remember we share a secret?"

Johnny Lightholder blushed to the roots of the hair for which Tamsin alone knew he used a hair restorer. "Just kiddin', Tamsin girl, heheh."

"Your sense of humour is going to catch you out one day. In fact," she turned round to him as the revelation struck her, "in fact ... it'll be your warped sense of humour that caused you to send out those Valentine cards, am I right?" She plopped Moonbeam down on the floor so she could put her hands on her hips.

"Oh, er, I, er ... me?" blathered Johnny. He was normally so full of himself, but since the business with the mountain bike murder he'd been quite afraid of Tamsin.

"Yes, you. I think it's just the sort of thing you'd find funny."

Johnny squirmed, while Mark's mouth fell open and he gaped like a fish.

Johnny scraped the ground with the toe of his boot, waved his arms for a moment, then folded them across his thin chest. "What if I did?"

"Oh dear," sighed Tamsin. "If you only knew how much you've upset people!"

"It were just a laugh."

"Not if you are a female of a certain age and you receive a card which says 'you've no hope'."

"I never said that!"

"Then, if it was you who sent them, who did?"

"I were drunk, weren't I," said Johnny plaintively, now well and truly up to his neck in it. "We was at the pub. An' I found a pack of Valentine cards wedged behind a cushion, didn't I. Must've been there for months. An' I'd found a list of all the folk who'd bought tickets for that Midsummer Valentine thing. Thought it'd be a laugh to send them. And one of the others said, 'here, give me that list you found, I'll send 'em for you.' Johnny gulped and looked shifty, wondering if this story was being believed, then carried on. "And I gev her the guest list I'd found in the shop when I was getting me fags, and let her get on with it." He looked up at her, his blue eyes wide, "I'd forgotten all about it. I were off my head with booze. It weren't me!"

"Right. You expect me to believe that?" Tamsin scowled at him.

"As it happens, it's the truth."

Mark giggled quietly.

"You wouldn't know the truth if it came and knocked your teeth out, Johnny Lightholder!"

She gazed on the bowed head of the silly chump who thought he was so great. "I'm going to let the police know who sent these odious poison Valentines. They'll be very glad to clear it up. In fact, one of them has a personal interest. You targeted someone special to him. I hope that doesn't cloud his judgment ..."

"Listen, Miss, er - Tamsin," Johnny hopped from foot to foot, narrowly missing Moonbeam's tiny paws as she also hopped from foot to foot in front of Tamsin. "Look, it was just a few old bats .."

It was now Tamsin's turn to fold her arms across her chest.

"Ok," he said, at last realising he was on a sticky wicket. "I'll see nobody else gets a card. I'm bringing a gel to that dance ..."

Tamsin interrupted him. "I'm not sure you'll be welcome on the night. We can refund your ticket."

Johnny's face fell as he was clearly in danger of losing credibility with his new girlfriend. "Tell you what," he said nervously, "I'll come and move tables or something. Make myself useful. Blow up balloons, sweep the floor .. Will that do?"

"Can you assure me that no more cards will be sent? Of any kind? To anyone?"

"Er. Yeah. I'll see to it. Actually, I think they ran out ..."

Tamsin nodded. "You and I both know it was you, Johnny, never mind your daft story. But if you can give me that assurance, that no more cards will be sent, then I'll tell the police that the person responsible has been found and is suitably remorseful, and will be performing some community service on the day of the Midsummer Valentine by way of reparation. Yes?"

He nodded silently, like a naughty six-year-old who'd been caught with his hand in the sweet-jar.

"Ok, then I'll tell Saffron that you'll arrive at the marquee at Malvern Springs Farm at 10 o'clock on the day, ready to do whatever she needs doing. I'm sure she'll have finished with you in time for you to go home and get ready. If you want to keep your tickets, you'll need to be prompt at 10. I mean it. I'll be checking."

Johnny turned towards the shop door, his shoulders bent - a different figure from the one who had strutted in a few minutes earlier. He stopped and turned. He tried to say something, but if it was 'sorry' or 'thank you', the words stuck in his throat. He lifted his hands and dropped them again, and shuffled out of the shop.

"Wow!" exclaimed Mark, his eyes wide. "I seen you do it again! How do you do it? It was like my Mum telling him off."

"I'm not quite like your Mum, nice though she is, Mark. I just can't stand nastiness, or injustice." She scooped Moonbeam up again and held her close. "It's what drives me, I think. That's why I do what I do with *Top Dogs*. I can't change the whole world, but I can change one dog-owner at a time." She grinned and gave Moonbeam a kiss on the top of her head.

"Don't forget to pin up one of those flyers, Mark!" And she too left the shop, with a tear in her eye.

CHAPTER TWENTY-FIVE

"Johnny Lightholder! Would you credit it!" Emerald took a sip of her green tea and beamed at Feargal, who was just arriving at the café table with a tray laden with toasted sandwiches and cakes.

"Oh, I would!" Charity nodded sagely. "That family seems to function entirely without morals. He can't help it. In fact, he's doing fairly well on the whole, given the start he had. They were brought up as thieving rascals, the lot of them."

Tamsin grabbed the nearest plate, which bore a mountain of red cake and whipped cream, with chocolate curls sliding off the top of it. "Oh my, this looks fantastic!" She took a mouthful and leant back in her chair, eyes closed. "Mmm. Sensational."

"So you've solved the Valentine mystery all on your own, and all you can think of is cake?" demanded Feargal, with a grin.

"It's scrumptious. I'm sure the Furies would reckon I have my priorities right. Aren't you having any?"

Tall, slender yogi Emerald smiled indulgently at her friend and her plate of cake. "Feargal eats for two," she grinned. She unwound and rewound her legs under her. As a yogi she was able to do extraordinary things with her limbs. "What did the Sergeant say when you told him? Didn't he want to arrest Johnny?"

"I think in the canon of crime it's fairly minor. They don't need to clutter up the court system more than is necessary."

"I suppose that's true, but I do think he should get his knuckles rapped."

"I think a day with Saffron organising the event will be punishment enough. Can you imagine the chaos?" They all nodded sadly. "But the Sergeant is telling everyone who reported a card, and assuring them it wasn't personal and they should forget it. Just someone messing about, a prankster."

"I expect they'll be relieved," said Charity, surreptitiously passing the end of her biscuit to Muffin, who sat beside the diminutive figure on the armchair, hoping for such luck. "So it's all plain sailing now for Saffron! The trouble is averted!"

"I'm not so sure," Tamsin licked the spoon and put it down ruefully on her empty plate. "This latest thing we uncovered involves people who are all due to come to the Midsummer Valentine. I think we're not out of the woods yet."

"Tell me again just where we're at, dear, I've rather lost track ..."

"These three men who were organising the scam were scheduled to come to Saffron's event. Two of them got tickets, remember? Michael was to bring his wife, and Jefferson was coming with Lucinda. And the whole thing is happening at Bill Lett's farm."

"Surely they won't come?" Charity looked aghast.

"I've heard nothing to say they're not coming. They haven't been arrested or anything yet. The police are doing a thorough investigation, so it may take a while."

"I guess Michael is trying to save face in advance of the inevitable trial." Feargal had finished his pile of toasties and was rejoining the conversation.

"And Jefferson? I wonder if Lucinda will entertain him, now she knows what sort of person he is," said Emerald.

Tamsin nodded and shrugged her shoulders. "I can only hope the scales have fallen from her eyes."

"And as for Bill Lett - he'll need every penny he can get his hands on now his get-rich-quick scheme has been dismantled," agreed Feargal.

"Saffron has been on to him. She rang me in a flap yesterday, and I told her just to straight out pin him down." Tamsin licked her fingers as she ate the last chocolate curl, "Mmm. You know the Furies are providing the desserts for her event? Can't wait ... And our deceitful farmer assures her it's full steam ahead. Everything's due to arrive on Friday and Saturday - the marquee and flooring, the furniture, glasses, crockery, and all the rest."

"But aren't the police arresting them over the abduction?" demanded Charity.

Feargal answered for Tamsin. "This noble nutcase absolutely refuses to press charges."

"But why, dear? Shouldn't they be hauled over the coals for what they did?"

"In a way, yes. But I don't want the name of *Top Dogs* dragged through the murk. Mud sticks, you know. And I don't want to waste energy on months of going over and over it again and again. It's done. Gone. Over. We move on."

"You're right, my dear. It's all about moving on." The old lady paused, nodding her head thoughtfully. "Moving on is important ..." and before anyone could press her to say more, she added quickly, "And I hear that you have some plans, am I right?" her eyes twinkled mischievously.

"You're a witch, so you are, Charity Cleveland! How on earth did you know? No, don't answer!" laughed Tamsin, and then proceeded to outline the ideas for the new home for her dog training school. Charity was delighted to see her enthusiasm, and once she'd ascertained that the Nether Trotley and Malvern classes would still continue, she said, "Well, that should keep you out of trouble, my dear!"

Feargal, who had now also polished off his treacle tart and clotted cream, said, "I was wondering. Will people travel to Jonathan's Cidery? I mean, will you lose people, it being out of town?"

"I'd thought about that too. But, you see, it's halfway from here to Hereford, so that opens up a new audience! The training will be fairly specialised in the main - for people who want to do more with their dogs than just the basics - so I think people will be happy to travel. After all, it's only twenty minutes from here. I'll still have my feeder classes for puppies and new rescue dogs. And now I'll have follow-on training to offer them!" She took another drink of her coffee. "And I do have some firm fans, you know! They've been asking when they can learn to do what I do with my dogs."

"Ready-made audience," Feargal nodded approvingly. "You've got it all worked out!"

"Ooh!" said Emerald, "You'll be able to announce it in your monthly *Malvern Mercury* piece!"

"Thanks, Em! I will! I hadn't thought of that." Tamsin reached across the table laden with coffee cups and empty plates and gave her friend a high five.

"You are celebrating, *mes amis?*" said the deep voice of Jean-Philippe, approaching the table with a tray and the ever-present tea-towel over his shoulder.

"New ventures!" said Tamsin gaily. "I've got plans for a new improved dog school out towards Hereford. Emerald and Feargal are planning a romantic getaway in the South of France .."

"Tamsin!" protested Emerald, as Feargal took her hand and smiled proudly.

".. and Charity has some idea - but she'll tell us in her own good time." She turned and smiled at her old friend.

Charity returned her smile shyly and put a hand on Muffin's head. "Thank you, dear. You're becoming quite the diplomat in your old age."

CHAPTER TWENTY-SIX

It was Saturday, and Tamsin awoke to a beautiful day and many wags and snuffles from her dogs, who were delighted that at last she was awake. She reached up to pull the curtain back a bit, and saw the sun shining on the Malverns behind her little house. The sky was a lustrous blue and there was not a wisp of cloud to be seen.

She stretched, gave Quiz a cuddle, and hopped out of bed, unaccustomedly full of beans and vigour, all her bruises and twinges now long gone. And downstairs she found Emerald upside down, her hands on the floor and her feet against the wall by the table.

"I'm glad you enjoy that," said Tamsin, heading for the kettle, "as I'm sure I wouldn't .. even if I could."

Emerald's legs floated down softly to the floor and she tossed her hair back as she became upright again. Opal was used to this nonsense, and remained purring on the counter, munching through her breakfast.

"I love it! Clears my head. Got anything on today?" asked Emerald. "Apart from tonight, I mean."

"You're right - it's the big day today. Big for Saffron, that is. Bit humdrum for me."

"I do hope it goes well for her. She's worked so hard."

"She's driven by her desire to make a good life for her little boy. There'll never be any help from his father, so she's making the best of it."

Tamsin loaded the cafetière with ground coffee, enjoying its scent. "And yes, I've got a couple of home visits today. The first one is to Bertie and Percy, the little Dachshunds. Remember them?"

"How could I forget them! They looked so cute at your Christmas *Top Dogs* party. Is there a problem with them?"

"Not particularly. Yvonne just needs a hand teaching them how to behave when visitors arrive. That's in Great Malvern. Then the next one is out Leigh Sinton way. I might drop in at Malvern Springs Farm on the way back. See how they're getting on."

"Rather you than me! I imagine Saffron will be totally frazzled."

And Emerald couldn't have been more right.

After an enjoyable session with Yvonne and her Dachsies, Tamsin went to the house in Leigh Sinton where someone had thought that adopting a two-year-old Malinois-Saluki cross was a good idea, and who - after an initial lesson - Tamsin quickly signed up for a course of sessions to help them manage the youngster's more unpredictable behaviour. She clambered back into her van with a big sigh, and arrived at Bill Lett's farm.

There was no sign of the farmer himself, she was glad to see, and she drove into the field where she found Johnny driving flags into the ground to mark out the car park area. As she got out of the car, he straightened up and mopped his brow.

"If I've moved them tables once, I've moved them a hundred times," he groused. "And I've had to re-do all these poles already. Saffron can't make up her mind."

"I think she's the sort of person who has to see things to know whether they're right. This is good for your soul, Johnny."

He snorted, and waved his lump hammer in the air with a shrug.

"But good for you showing up. I'm sure Saffron has been very glad of your help," Tamsin added, sincerely.

"There won't be any more about this?" he looked up under his long childish lashes.

"Not from me, for sure. And I gather the Sergeant is happy that he's been able to put people's minds at rest and mark another case closed."

"You gev him my name?" said Johnny sharply.

"No. He wanted to know, of course .. but I didn't tell him, Johnny."

"Ah. Thanks, Miss." Johnny turned and squinted at North Hill, the end of the Hills that can be seen from that side of town. "Well, I best get on," he said with the hint of a smile and something of a spring in his step, and set about banging another pole into the ground.

Tamsin gasped as she entered the marquee. It was a fairyland of light and sound. Saffron, her curly hair a massive tangled bush which represented well what was inside her head, was directing a remarkably patient electrician where she wanted the strings of lights, and Manic was testing his disco equipment in his corner, with lots of black boxes and cables snaking all over the floor.

He waved at her and turned off the noise. "Don't you worry about the mess," he said, following her gaze. "All these cables will be safely tucked away soon enough. Don't want anyone tripping!"

"How's it going, Manic? I see Saffron's up to ninety."

"She'll be fine when it's all done. She cares, you see." He turned his brown eyes towards Saffron and his face softened. Tamsin nodded with a smile, and walked towards Saffron and the electrician.

"I was passing - just thought I'd drop in and see how it's going. It looks fantastic, Saffron!"

Saffron plunged forward and gave Tamsin a big hug, almost knocking her backwards. The electrician grasped his moment of freedom and shinned up his ladder to fiddle with cables and lights.

"You can't imagine!" Saffron pushed her hair back from her rosy cheeks. There's just so much to do. I can't thank you enough for sending Johnny over. I don't know what persuaded him to come, but he's a trooper! He's worked really hard. Oh, just a minute .." She grabbed her phone out of her pocket and said, "No, he doesn't like fish. I've told you before. Give him the bread and some tiny cubes of cheese and cucumber - that'll do him. Gotta go now." She snapped the phone shut with a frustrated gesture and dropped it back in her pocket. "It's so hard to find good minders .. I just wish I was at home more with Charlie."

"I see you have Manic helping too?"

"Oh, Manic! He's a dote, so he is." Her shoulders relaxed as she looked across to him. "I'm so relieved that Bill has let this all go ahead. There were an awful few days when I thought I may have to cancel everything again .."

"We'd have found you somewhere, don't worry. But has there been any trouble from any of those three men?"

"I haven't seen Bill at all, and I haven't heard a peep from the other two. I do hope there won't be any trouble tonight .." She chewed her lip.

"This how you wants it, Miss?" called a voice from the top of the ladder.

"Oh no, further over to the right!" Saffron spun round and raced back to the electrician, waving her arms like a windmill, and Tamsin reckoned she had done her bit of support and it was time to escape.

CHAPTER TWENTY-SEVEN

"Can you kind of twist it a bit, Emerald?"

"Hold on, let me put one of these tiny safety pins in .." Emerald sounded funny as she was talking with the pins in her mouth. "There you go! Now it's perfect!"

"Oh thanks, Em! Dressing in anything other than a fleece jumper and cargo pants is really not my thing. While you .." Tamsin stepped back to admire her friend. "You look ravishing."

Emerald blushed sweetly and fingered her ash-blonde hair, strands of which were tumbling down from her up-do.

"That turquoise really suits your colouring."

"Well, I think you look amazing in your royal blue velvet, Tamsin. Really. It shows off that you actually have a nice figure under all those baggy jumpers and jackets you usually wear."

"There's a benefit from all the walking I do .."

"Listen to us! A mutual admiration society in full swing. Hey! Is that a car pulling up?"

The dogs answered with welcoming woofs as the back door opened and in walked a very smart Feargal, and an equally dapper Jonathan. "Helloo?" they called up the stairs, while keeping the dogs at a slight distance to minimise the waft of hairs of every colour sticking to their black evening dress.

"Down in a mo," called Tamsin, and to Emerald, "That was a good idea to share the lift." She scooped up her long dress and stepped gingerly down the stairs. There were cries of "Wow!" from both their beaus as the two women came into view.

"No, Banjo! You mustn't even brush against me!" said Tamsin, bending over to give her grey and white dog a kiss on his head. "I'm wearing girls' clothes!"

"Girls' clothes!" laughed Emerald with a snort.

"And very lovely you look in them too," said Jonathan quietly.

Feargal, who had been busy goggling at Emerald, snapped out of it and said, "Jonathan's opted to drive, so he's on the lemonade."

"Funny thing about making alcoholic drinks for a living is that I don't particularly want to drink them when I'm out," he explained. Tamsin gave him a smile as he took her hand.

"Let's get going!" said Feargal. "We don't want to be too late. Saffron's presumably for the birds by now?"

"She certainly was when I dropped round there earlier. But I think Johnny Lightholder was a big help. He couldn't throw down his tools and walk out for fear of being reported over the Valentine cards. So he actually had to make sure the work was done before he could escape. I was quite impressed with him, actually."

"I think he's not a bad guy at heart. Just fighting against generations of inculcation with crime," said Feargal. "I wonder how he'll scrub up!" he grinned.

"And who his date is?" added Emerald.

And, after fond farewells to the dogs, and Opal, who - of course - remained aloof over the whole venture, contenting herself with pointing a back leg in the air and washing her bottom, they set off to Malvern Springs Farm.

There were a good number of cars in the field by the time they arrived, lined up correctly behind Johnny's flags, and the marquee looked inviting with all the fairy lights and the thump of Manic's music bouncing off the hedgerows. As they went in they felt the warmth of the noisy buzz of conversation, laughter, the clink of glasses, and the music.

"Look, there's Saffron over there - should we announce ourselves?" said Feargal.

"She looks pretty harassed," Emerald said. "But she's very striking in that black and red outfit."

"Let's catch her later," said Tamsin, "Oh hallo there .." And she was off to greet one of her dog class students.

"You look amazing, Tamsin!" said Yvonne, who for once had no Dachshunds in tow. "I always picture you in jumpers and jeans ..."

"You seem to have the ability to get anyone to walk to heel!" laughed Shirley - Mark Bendick's mother and another of her students - as she nodded a smile towards Jonathan, still standing with Feargal and Emerald.

"Perhaps," added 'Setterman' who regularly turned up to classes with a new English Setter and whose long name Tamsin could never remember, "you should have a *Top Dogs* Ball as well as a fancy dress party for the dogs!" and he laughed uproariously at his joke before inviting Shirley to "join me in a trot".

It wasn't long before Tamsin bumped into Saffron near the bar. "Any sign of those blokes?" she asked, quietly.

"The council geezer, Michael, was here earlier doing a 'Hail fellow, well met' act with everyone. But I think he felt frozen out and left early."

"Good. What about the other one?"

"Lucinda's over there," Saffron indicated the colourfully-dressed artist chatting with a rather more respectable-looking man than Jefferson. "She told me she'd told him to sling his hook! She's changed all her website details and passwords and that, and she's banished him from her life."

"That's really good news! I'll chat with her later."

Tamsin enjoyed herself a lot more than she had anticipated, dressy events not being her thing. In fact, if it weren't for Saffron, you wouldn't have caught her dead at one, as she said to her escort. Jonathan was very attentive, and patient while she chatted to so many people - what's more, he turned out to be a fine dancer too.

"Funny seeing you in a dinner suit instead of a check shirt and jeans!" Tamsin said as he swung her round and caught her again.

"I can tell you which I'm more comfortable in .."

"You and me both!" Tamsin grinned. She felt relaxed and actually enjoying the moment.

"There on the farm, me on my Fergie with Teal, you trotting about with all your dogs and your students .. I like the thought of that." He looked earnestly at her.

Tamsin's eyes grew round as she looked up at him. The room stilled for a moment as she looked carefully, as if for the first time. "Do you mean .."

But she didn't get the chance to finish her question, as a loud roar penetrated the music.

"It's my farm and I'll do what I want!" Bill Lett was standing in the middle of the floor, lurching unsteadily and snarling at the guests - who pulled away in alarm.

"Oh Lord, this was what I feared," said Tamsin.

"You're all a load of n-no-good time-washters," he cried out, waving his fist in the air. "You c'n all clear orf!"

Jonathan moved her behind him, saying, "Stay there," and looked for Feargal. But before he could get closer to the ranting farmer, the nice Sergeant who had accompanied Janice Carruthers stepped forward and said in clear tones, "Now now, Bill, let's get you home. You look as though you could do with another drink - got some in your farmhouse? Let's go and see."

He gestured to the exit, standing back to usher Bill out.

"I won't be told on my own land!" roared the drunken farmer. Then he turned and spoke confidentially to the Sergeant. "How can a man turn an honest penny? Farming is shot. No future. I tells ya, no future. I got a right to turn my hand to summat else. Diversery .. diverfy .. *diversify!* That's what we gotta do. Never mind all my skills with lambing and haymaking. I got to divert .. diverse .."

"Tell me about it! Same with us in the force. We used to just go out and catch robbers. Nowadays we have to work on computers, review video, type endless reports .." The Sergeant was subtly edging Bill towards the doorway.

"Forms! You never seen forms like the Min, the Minisry, the Department, has us fill in." Bill clapped the Sergeant on the shoulder. "You'll understand, won't you? I was jes' turning my hand to a new scheme - 'Green .. Green summat' they calls it. And now they're threatening me with jail - jail! I asks yer. All for trying to diversery, diver .. Fiddlesticks - do summat else."

The crowd, who had frozen in place as soon as Bill had launched his tirade, began to relax as the capable Sergeant ushered the drunken farmer through the entrance. He turned to wink at Janice and mouthed "Won't be long," as they walked off through the car park. Bill's rantings could still be heard inside, so Manic switched on a softer, cheerier piece of music, and got everyone dancing again, as the hubbub of conversation grew back.

"Well, I'll be," said Jonathan to Feargal who was now standing beside him. "That's skilful, that is."

Feargal nodded. "There's nothing like twenty years on the beat for honing your people skills. He's impressive, that one. Let's give him ten minutes then we can go and see if he needs any help."

"Ok," said Jonathan. "Bill may have fists like hams, but I don't think he wants to use them, for all his shouting. He's more likely to burst into tears."

Tamsin had tapped Emerald on the arm while all this was going on, and they were now over near the bar comforting a stricken Saffron.

"It's ok, Saffron, he's gone," Emerald said soothingly. "Do some of your yoga breathing - close your eyes and breathe in with me .."

"It's all over!" added Tamsin. "Look, Manic's sorting out the music to lift the mood. Bill won't be back."

Saffron was standing up straighter, her hands gripping Emerald's, her eyes closed, breathing deeply with her yoga teacher. Tamsin shook her head in wonder as the colour came back to Saffron's cheeks and her shoulders relaxed.

"Tell you what, Saffron. How about you go and talk to Janice? She may be worried, and now she's on her own for a bit."

They dispatched Saffron over to Janice, and Tamsin gave a deep sigh.

"Hey, that were cool!" Johnny Lightholder had bustled up beside Tamsin. He was wearing a white shirt with a frilly front and a bootlace tie and looked astonishingly smart."He's a bit of alright, that copper. My ole Dad used ta say .."

"I don't know if your old Dad's words would fit the bill here, Johnny," said a chirpy voice from just behind him.

"Rosie!" said Tamsin in surprise. "Good to see you - you look lovely, out of your Health Shop overalls. You with Johnny?"

"I am so." Rosie turned and gave Johnny a cheeky grin. "He worked ever so hard today, gettin' all this ready."

"He did. I'm impressed, Johnny."

"You won't be taking it further?" asked Rosie earnestly.

"Can't remember why I recommended you to help Saffron now ..." Tamsin looked vague. "But I'm glad I did."

Johnny went to clap Tamsin on the shoulder, thought better of it, and grabbed Rosie's hand instead. He tapped his forehead in a mock salute, and pulled his girl to the dance floor. "Look, they're doing that cowboy dancing thing .."

And Sara appeared, grabbing Emerald and Tamsin each by the wrist, "It's a line dance! You have to join in - come on!" Feargal, Jonathan, and Andrew were similarly dragged on to the floor - and they all joined in with gusto. Tamsin enjoyed it rather more than she'd expected.

As the party drew to a close, Manic set up a playlist of smoochy music and took the opportunity to abandon his decks to lead Saffron to the dance floor - to applause from many of the assembled guests.

And so the evening ended without further incident.

Unless you count when Jonathan grabbed one of the big red heart-shaped balloons and whispered to Tamsin, "Tamsin Kernick, I adore you. Will you marry me?"

CHAPTER TWENTY-EIGHT

"Mais, alors!" said Jean-Philippe as he took everyone's order. "You look a very happy bunch today." It was coming towards the end of summer, and everyone had been busy doing summery things.

"We are, Jean-Philippe!" responded Tamsin, waving her hand as she spoke, so she could admire the light glinting off her ring. "Not only did we solve two crimes a while ago, and helped Saffron make a success of her new venture, but we have some happy outcomes too."

"I hear you had a near squeak this time, *Mademoiselle* Tamsin. Do you think this is a warning?"

Emerald jumped in. "We keep telling her that."

"And more importantly," said Charity, *"Jonathan* keeps telling her that. I think this new move is all a plan to keep Tamsin out of further trouble!"

"You'll be too busy with your new business plan, *eh bien?"*

"I certainly will! I can't wait to get started." Tamsin looked round her group of friends and beamed at them. "I have lovely friends. They look out for me."

Feargal snorted. "Just as well someone does, Missis. You need to be looked out for. You're a liability!"

"Et pour vous?" Jean-Philippe brandished the pen over his order book and raised his black bushy eyebrows at Feargal.

"My order?" Feargal raised just the one eyebrow and grinned.

"Mais non! You and *Mademoiselle* Emerald have some plans, if I am not much mistaken?"

Feargal put his hand over Emerald's. "There's no flies on you, Jean-Philippe!" he laughed. "Yes, we realised on our Pyrenean holiday that we were made for each other! So I'm moving into Pippin Lane with Emerald - once Tamsin's removed all her pesky dogs!"

Tamsin covered Quiz's ears. "He doesn't mean it, Quizzy. He loves you really."

"I do. The place will be very different without them there."

"You're buying the house?" asked Jean-Philippe, as he tore off the order page and handed it to Kylie, who had appeared beside him. She gave a big grin and spun on her heel, her tiny pink skirt and her matching pink hair swinging round as she headed to the counter to start on the coffees.

"Renting it," said Feargal.

Tamsin sighed. "Jonathan insists I keep it on. I think he's worried he'll change his mind and then he won't be able to get rid of me!"

Charity leaned forward. "I think he's being very sensible. That house is your asset, and you never know what the future holds. Things can change, you know. I mean - there may come a time when you want to use the money from a sale."

"You don't think I'm going to be evicting Feargal and Emerald and moving back in?"

"Absolutely not! As I told you my dear, Jonathan is a *keeper.*" Charity leant back in her chair and stroked Muffin's ears.

"I see you've been to the Farmers' Market today." Jean-Philippe nodded in the direction of the bulging shopping bags propped against the wall, with rhubarb and the silver tassels of corn cobs poking out of the top, and large sourdough loaves threatening to fall out of their tissue paper wrappings. "Is Jonathan coming over to join you?"

"He'll drop over for an express espresso, yes, when Manic turns up to mind the stall."

Jean-Philippe gave a deep bow. "I will look out for him. He is a brave man," and with a wink he drifted away to greet the newcomers at the next table.

They had to move the chairs around once more when they were joined by Andrew and Sara, who, as usual, was bubbly and happy.

"So, tell me all!" said Sara. "We're just back from an activity holiday in the Peak District - climbing and walking mostly," she grinned at Andrew. "And apart from the drama at the Midsummer Valentine, I'm out of the loop. Last thing I knew was that someone was sending Vinegar Valentines to people. Did you find out who that was?"

"And why they were doing it?" added Andrew.

"We did. It turned out to be Johnny Lightholder - but I promised him I wouldn't report him if he helped Saffron on the day."

"And did he?"

"He was excellent. Put up with a lot to save his skin."

"So why did he send them?" persisted Andrew.

"It was just a mindless, drunken, prank," sighed Tamsin.

"There was nothing personal in it," said Emerald. "He just picked women's names off the guest list that Saffron had managed to lose, and wrote nasty things."

"Fancy telling Niamh O'Connor that she had no hope!" said Feargal. "She's a lovely young woman. Just shows he didn't have a clue who these people he was hurting were."

"And you didn't report him to the police?" asked Sara in wonderment.

"Didn't see the point," Tamsin picked up her coffee mug. "As it happens, once they had an idea who it was they were able to make some partial finger-print matches off the cards - but not enough to be conclusive. Johnny's the sort of person who's on the fence between crime and being a useful member of society. I didn't want to push him further over the wrong side! I thought it salutary for him to spend a day being nagged to death by Saffron instead."

"Presumably a lesson learnt! He won't want to go through that again," chuckled Andrew.

"But he was useful, as it happened," said Charity, as ever ready to rush to the Lightholders' defence.

"Yes, Saffron gave him a special mention in that little speech she gave halfway through, and called him over to shake his hand."

"Rosie clung to him - she was tickled pink, especially with all the photos being taken," laughed Emerald.

"One actually found its way into the report in the *Malvern Mercury!*" said Feargal.

More chairs had to be shuffled around and more coffees ordered as Jonathan raced into The Cake Stop. He gave Tamsin a kiss on the cheek, saying, "Just got fifteen minutes. It's pretty busy today in this lovely weather, and Manic has hedgehogs to feed and re-home."

"It's great that he's able to help you out on the stand," said Charity.

"Tit for tat really. He'll be coming round to the orchard later to release another hedgehog. And a little bird tells me that Saffron and young Charlie are coming for the outing too."

"Lovely that they get on so well," said Charity. "Young Saffron deserves someone reliable and kind." Everyone nodded and looked pleased.

"Manic is a case of 'You *can't* judge a book by its cover!'" said Emerald.

"And I expect you'll have a happy half hour talking about Fergie tractors!" Tamsin grinned.

"Goes without saying," laughed Jonathan. "I'm sure Charlie will enjoy that too!"

"Aren't tractors dangerous?" asked Emerald.

"Don't worry, he won't be near it when it's running. I can sit him on my lap on the seat while the engine's off. Can't be too careful with children and farm vehicles," he smiled at Tamsin, a kind of secret smile.

"Tamsin was just telling us that you don't want her to sell Pippin Lane," prompted Charity.

"I don't want her to lose her home. I want her to feel free and able to leave whenever she wants to." He turned to Tamsin, "You're like a wild thing, and you must be free to make your own choice."

"Hmm, that sounds just like how I work with dogs!" said Tamsin, her eyes sparkling.

"So what was that rampaging farmer on about, then?" asked Andrew into the sudden silence, still keen to catch up.

"Oh that!" said Tamsin.

"You have Tamsin to thank for uncovering a nasty fraud," said Jonathan.

"And you have my dogs to thank for rescuing me when I was kidnapped!"

"NO!" chorused Sara and Andrew.

Tamsin stroked Quiz's head which was by one knee, and fondled Banjo's ears as he gazed adoringly at her. Moonbeam was happily lying down playing bitey-face with Muffin and too busy to pay attention.

"You see, I learnt some things, overheard some things, thought out some things .. and joined up the dots. Turns out Bill Lett, the farmer you saw rather worse for wear at the Midsummer Valentine, was colluding with Michael Cummings in the Council Planning Division, and Jefferson Smyth who was using the artist Lucinda Fry's website as cover - well, these three were in a scheme to defraud the government of hundreds of thousands of pounds."

"How?"

"A green energy scam. Claiming massive grants for something they never planned to go through with. I believe Jefferson and Michael were thinking of disappearing to South America or the Caribbean or somewhere. No idea how Bill Lett proposed to avoid imprisonment."

"And that's where all three of 'em will be going!" said Feargal with pleasure. "Clink!"

"But what about this - *kidnapping?*" Sara looked appalled.

"I decided to take the long view. I was safe. They're going inside for a long time for the other crime. That'll do me."

"And I guess you don't want to be looking over your shoulder if you get them banged up then they get early release in a few years .." said Andrew thoughtfully.

"Very true," said Jonathan. "We want a peaceful life. It's apples and dogs for us, all the way!" he beamed at Tamsin, then at the rest of them.

Kylie appeared with their top-up order, and they busied themselves passing mugs round.

"And cake! Look who's just arrived!"

And across the room came Damaris Dodds, the youngest and very definitely the smallest of the three sisters who made up Dodds & Co, aka The Three Furies. She was carrying a large cake box.

"A little bird told me there were special celebrations to be made," she said, as she lowered the cake box to the table. Kylie, who had been forewarned, appeared with a large knife and a stack of plates.

"Oh, Damaris, it's lovely!" exclaimed Emerald, as the box was opened and she saw the intertwined letters F and E, and J and T piped on the top of the royal icing, along with a white marzipan cat and four marzipan dogs.

"I did get your dog right, I hope, Jonathan?" said Damaris anxiously.

"Oh, that's Teal alright!" Jonathan looked really chuffed. Seeing the cake made his new life seem more real than ever. "You've got his brown ears bang on!"

"That is so kind of you, Damaris - do thank Penelope and Electra for us," said Tamsin, already licking some icing off her finger.

"We have to look after our special people," Damaris replied. "Yes, dear, that would be very nice," she said to Kylie who had suggested tea.

Once they were all enjoying their coffees, teas, and cakes, Charity said, "I invited a visitor to join us this morning too."

"Oh yes? Who is it?" asked Tamsin eagerly.

"A very dear old friend .. and here she is!" She waved vigorously as an old lady stepped through the door being held open for her by Jean-Philippe.

"Oh, it's Dorothy!" said Tamsin, gesturing to Feargal to draw up yet another chair.

Jean-Philippe bent to greet the red golden retriever walking nicely beside her. "And what is your name, young *chien?*"

"This is Toffee!" said Dorothy with pride as she turned to return Charity's wave and came over to join the group.

"Hiya Toffee!" Tamsin greeted the excited young dog and introduced him to his playmates Quiz, Banjo, and Moonbeam, who were lying on their mats in the soft sunshine coming in the window, the shadows from The Cake Stop lettering curling over their bodies. Turning back to Dorothy she said, "Eddie not up to the walk?"

"No dear, he's getting so doddery now. He's ok on the flat, but these Malvern hills are too much for him. He's quite happy snoozing in the kitchen with the bone I left him. And he'll be delighted to see Toffee when we come back. That worked out so well .. in the end." She paused for a moment. "Especially with our latest plan." She turned to Charity, "Have you told them yet, dear?"

"Not yet. I thought I'd wait till you arrived," said the diminutive old lady, who was now sharing her armchair with Muffin perched beside her.

"Plan?" asked Emerald.

"You two are cooking something up?" said Feargal.

"Spill the beans - immediately!" demanded impatient Tamsin.

"Well, my dears - with all this moving about and new lives starting, I thought it would be the right time for me to move and start a new life."

Tamsin looked crestfallen. "You're moving away?"

Dorothy patted her hand, "Just hear her out, Tamsin."

"Patience is definitely not your strong suit, Tamsin, my dear! You see, I'm finding the upkeep of my little cottage in Nether Trotley increasingly burdensome. I'm not so agile with home repairs as I was. And honestly, " she sighed, "I enjoy tending my vegetable garden, but clambering up a ladder to fix the roof or the guttering .."

"No, you shouldn't!" exclaimed Emerald.

"You're right, I shouldn't."

"And I've been finding running my little B&B gets harder too," put in Dorothy. "All that bed-making and hoovering .. I'd rather be reading a book or walking the dogs."

"You and me both," murmured Tamsin with a smile.

"So we put our heads together, and did some sums .. rather a lot of sums, actually .. and we've decided to move to that new development out towards Worcester."

"The assisted living place?"

"Malvern View, or something?"

"That's right, dears, Malvern View Village. They call it a 'retirement village'."

"Where they have lots of apartments and a café and swimming pool and gardens and the like?" said Feargal. "We covered their grand opening a couple of years ago."

"That's it, and they do all the servicing and maintenance for you," nodded Dorothy.

"And they let you have dogs and cats?" Tamsin's eyes widened as she closed in on the most important detail.

"They do! That was an essential for us, of course. And there's no limit on how many you can have," said Charity. "We enquired at some places where they said you can bring a pet, but you can't 'replace' it." Charity gazed fondly at Muffin. "Well, we all know you can't 'replace' an animal, but I understood what they meant."

"But this place is different?" Tamsin asked anxiously.

"It is! No pet limit!"

Tamsin let her breath out and relaxed a little.

"Will you not find it hard to adapt to an apartment after both having your own homes and gardens for so long?" Emerald asked.

"This is the beauty of it!" Charity began, getting quite animated. "The original old house and its other houses are divided up into apartments, and the new building is for the café and library and swimming pool and lounges .."

"And we're getting a whole house to ourselves!" Dorothy squeaked, unable to keep it to herself any longer.

"That's right! We're so lucky. They'd just finished renovating the former gardener's cottage. It's quite separate and has its own little garden at the back."

"And the front! We'll get the best of both worlds!" enthused Dorothy.

"We get the privacy of our own home, complete with a garden for the animals .."

".. where we can grow things .."

"And everything is looked after for us."

"It sounds wonderful, Charity!" said Tamsin. "But will you keep your car? Will we still see you in Malvern?"

"Oh, we won't be far away, dears. And I'll definitely still want to come to the Farmers' Market for a lot of what we eat. And I'll still be doing my literacy sessions at the Library."

"And the knitting classes at the school?" asked Emerald.

"And the church choir?" added Jonathan.

"I will - not to mention your Tricks Class in Nether Trotley - couldn't miss that! And I'll have more energy too. You'll have to come and visit us when we get there."

"Oh, we'd love to! Wouldn't we, guys?" she turned to look at all her friends who nodded enthusiastically. "But .. I'd heard these sort of places are terribly expensive?"

"And will you have to wait ages while you sell your cottage, Charity?" Feargal added.

"It's all in hand! I'm going to rent out my cottage. Can't bring myself to part with the place where I was born."

"And I can easily sell my place right in the centre of Great Malvern - either as a home or as a going concern as a B&B."

"That, and some money I, er, discovered, will be enough," added Charity cryptically.

"You discovered some money? How? Where?" demanded Tamsin.

"You taking to a life of crime, Charity?" quipped Feargal.

"I wish I could 'discover' some too!" said Andrew.

"Don't worry, it's all above board," Charity assured them. "In fact, it's rather an amazing story, how I, in my farm labourer's cottage, came by enough money to buy a grand new property."

"But how?" demanded Tamsin.

"Well, my dear, you're going to have to be patient. I *will* tell you exactly how it happened .. but I'm going to string you along for a bit longer." Charity smiled smugly, and gave Dorothy a wink.

Dorothy grinned, wiggled her shoulders and made a zip sign across her mouth.

"Charity! You're incorrigible!" shouted Tamsin, with such force that all five dogs looked at her expectantly.

Whatever was happening, it seemed that their people were very happy about it. And they were happy to go along with anything that made their people happy.

Want to know Charity's secret? How she managed to lay hands on hundreds of thousands of pounds for her new venture? You can find out all about it, and what the future holds for Tamsin, in Book 1 of the new series, *The Charity and Muffin English Cozy Mysteries*, here:

https://mybook.to/TailVillageMurder

Meanwhile, to catch up with how Tamsin first came to live in Malvern, read *Where it all began* here https://urlgeni.us/Lucyemblemcozy

And if you've enjoyed these books - and especially this one - I'd love it if you could leave a brief review at the store where you bought it so that others may enjoy the stories and be kind to their animals too. See you in the next book!

ABOUT LUCY

From an early age I loved animals. From doing "showjumping" in the back garden with Simon, the long-suffering family pet - many years before Dog Agility was invented - I worked in the creative arts till I came back to my first love and qualified as a dog trainer.

Working for years with thousands of dogs and their colourful owners - from every walk of life - I found that their fancies and foibles, their doings and their undoings, served to inspire this series of cozy mysteries.

While the varying characters weave their way through the books, some becoming established personnel in the stories, the stars of the show are the animals!

They don't have human powers. They don't need to. They have plenty of powers of their own, which need only patience and kindness to bring out and enjoy with them.

If you enjoyed this story, I would LOVE it if you could hop over to where you purchased your book and leave a brief review! So that others may enjoy Tamsin's stories and be kind to their animals.

Lucy Emblem

facebook.com/lucyemblemcozies

instagram.com/lucyemblem

bookbub.com/authors/lucy-emblem

tiktok.com/@lucyemblem

pinterest.com/LucyEmblemCozyMysteries

ALL LUCY EMBLEM'S COZY ENGLISH MYSTERIES

Where it all began ..

https://urlgeni.us/Lucyemblemcozy

Sit, Stay, Murder! *

https://mybook.to/SitStayMurder

Ready, Aim, Woof! *

https://mybook.to/ReadyAimWoof

Down Dog! *

https://mybook.to/downdog

Barks, Bikes, and Bodies! *

https://mybook.to/BarksBikesBodies

Ma-ah, Ma-ah, Murder! *

https://mybook.to/TamsinKernickCozies

Snapped and Framed! *

https://mybook.to/SnappedFramed

Christmas Carols and Canine Capers! A Howling Good Christmas Mystery! *

https://mybook.to/Christmascozy

Game, Set, and Catch! *

https://mybook.to/GameSetCatch

A Howl Lot of Love and Lies!

https://mybook.to/HowlLotofLove

The Charity and Muffin Cozy English Mystery series

A Tail of Village Murder

https://mybook.to/TailVillageMurder

* Also available in Large Print

https://mybook.to/TamsinKernickCozies

Printed in Dunstable, United Kingdom